MW01143843

Career soldier C love could be lost in the blink of an eye, leaving an empty place that was just another pothole on life's rocky road. The detours of sudden single fatherhood and a nosy best friend who won't let even death stop her from interferring in every date leave Christie convinced that finding a partner is next to impossible.

State Trooper Robert Lindstrom catches Christie speeding along the stretch of highway he patrols and a routine traffic stop turns into love lights flashing and instant attraction for these two men in uniform. It looks like smooth sailing to their happily ever after until an unexpected deployment sends Christie into danger. Can their love survive both bombs and the betrayal of Christie by his closest comrade?

MLR PRESS AUTHORS

Featuring a roll call of some of the best writers of gay erotica and mysteries today!

Derek Adams	Z. Allora	Maura Anderson
Victor J. Banis	Jeanne Barrack	Laura Baumbach
Ally Blue	J.P. Bowie	Barry Brennessel
Michael Breyette	Nowell Briscoe	P.A. Brown
Jade Buchanan	James Buchanan	Charlie Cochrane
Karenna Colcroft	Jamie Craig	Kirby Crow
Ethan Day	Diana DeRicci	Jason Edding
Theo Fenraven	Angela Fiddler	S.J. Frost
Kimberly Gardner	Michael Gouda	Roland Graeme
Storm Grant	Amber Green	LB Gregg
Kaje Harper	Jan Irving	David Juhren
Kiernan Kelly	M. King	Matthew Lang
J.L. Langley	Josh Lanyon	Anna Lee
Elizabeth Lister	Clare London	William Maltese
Z.A. Maxfield	Timothy McGivney	Lloyd A. Meeker
Patric Michael	AKM Miles	Reiko Morgan
Jet Mykles	William Neale	Cherie Noel
Willa Okati	Neil S. Plakcy	Jordan Castillo Price
Luisa Prieto	Rick R. Reed	A.M. Riley
George Seaton	Jardonn Smith	Caro Soles
JoAnne Soper-Cook	Richard Stevenson	Liz Strange
Marshall Thornton	Lex Valentine	Maggie Veness
Haley Walsh	Missy Welsh	Stevie Woods
Lance Zarimba		

Check out titles, both available and forthcoming, at
www.mlrpress.com

THE SOLDIER
& THE STATE
TROOPER

CHERIE NOEL

mlrpress

www.mlrpress.com

Copyright 2011 by Cherie Noel

Published by
MLR Press, LLC
3052 Gaines Waterport Rd.
Albion, NY 14411

Visit ManLoveRomance Press, LLC on the Internet:
www.mlrpress.com

Cover Art by Winterheart Designs
Editing by Jennifer Ayres

Print format ISBN# 978-1-60820-402-1
ebook format ISBN#978-1-60820-403-8

Issued 2011

Dedication

This first one's for Jambie Jo and the Eros Ladies...and they know why.

It's also for Patric Michael; he will always be my Balthazar.

PART ONE: FALLING IN

Christie stretched his arms over his head, arching his back languorously. Mmmm. The sun on his face felt so good. It was warm and light like a gentle touch. It...

Sunlight. On his face.

Oh God. He was going to be late signing out on leave.

Christie flung himself off the bed toward his closet. He grabbed the first pair of jeans he could lay his hands on. Thank God he didn't need to be in uniform. There wasn't time to iron one. He'd already missed the 0630 Physical Training formation. If he made it to the base before the 0900 formation he might skate by with just dirty looks from First Sergeant Bartone.

If the first sergeant didn't decide to give him an article fifteen.

Crap. If Christie got that, he'd end up losing his leave as well. He could barely afford the gas to get to work now. An article fifteen would cut his pay in half for forty-five days.

Christie yanked a favorite soft green oversized sweater off the back of the closet door. First Sergeant Bartone was a stickler for his troops being on time. The last man to earn the first sergeant's ire over a lack of timeliness had been a big mechanic named Ingals. The poor guy had to wear a wall clock around his neck for a week as his "corrective action" for being thirty seconds late to Physical Training. Considering how late Christie was running, the first sergeant could easily give him extra duty.

A few months before, that would have just been something for his buddy Evans to kid him about afterwards. Now-

A sharp wail echoed from the other room.

Frankie.

Christie pulled on his jeans. If he got extra duty, he wouldn't be able to pick up Frankie from daycare before it closed. The daycare charged you a buck a minute for being late. After fifteen minutes they called social services on you, and your chain of command. Christie shuddered. That would suck big hairy donkey balls.

The first thing First Sergeant Bartone would ask would be why he hadn't activated his family care plan. Sure. Like Aunt Cate could just give up her life for forty-five days to come out here and hold his hand. Ha! Like he'd even ask her to after all she'd already given up to raise him after his parents died.

The first thing social services would ask would be if he had a history of abandoning his daughter.

So.

Yes.

Once.

But how was he supposed to know Evans's beater was going to break down on the way back from their errand in town? He'd run the two miles back to post in twelve minutes flat. Best time ever. Too bad it wasn't on a physical training test. At least it got him back before the worker called Child Protective Services.

Christie didn't go anywhere in Evans's car anymore. They took Christie's brand new, very reliable Neon if they had to run an errand in town for their squad leader or the platoon sergeant.

He threw his sweater over his head. Pulling socks up as he stumbled across the hallway, he fell through Frankie's door. Miss Kitty, a calico short hair that adopted his little family the day they moved into their new military housing, peeked at him through the slats of his daughter's crib.

"Good morning Miss Kitty…I have to grab Frankie and run honey, but I promise I'll be back in just a little while with your breakfast."

Great. Now he was talking to the cat. Christie really needed to find a sitter and get out of the house once in a while.

Scooping Frankie out of her crib, Christie took a moment to snuggle her warm sleep-sweet little body against his chest. He pressed his nose into her silky black curls and breathed in her baby smell. Nobody had ever told him he'd get addicted to the way she smelled. To be fair, Carolyn and Lisa hadn't had time.

Christie was supposed to be the happy go lucky poppa who visited once a year when he was on leave and sent lavish birthday presents. Caro and Liss knew how to be moms. What did he know?

Blinking rapidly, Christie hurried over to the changing table. He quickly stripped Frankie out of her sleeper and sopping-wet diaper. Once her little bottom was clean, dry, and again encased in a diaper, he popped her into a butter-yellow onesie. Tiny little matching pants followed by even smaller socks a moment later completed the outfit. Christie checked the diaper bag's contents against the list he'd gotten from his Aunt Cate to be sure it was stocked for emergencies. Everything was squared away like a baby first sergeant was coming to inspect. Christie gave himself a little pat on the back.

Frankie started to fuss, so he slid his hand under her to pick her up from the changing table. It slid in a warm gooey mush that coated the table's surface. Christie closed his eyes and prayed for strength. Today was laundry day. He dug around in the diaper bag. Coming up with a mismatched pair of red pants with yellow ducks on them and an orange shirt with big purple polka dots on it, he resigned himself to carting around the world's tiniest clown.

At least she wasn't wearing a big red clown nose.

Though that would have made Caro laugh till she peed on herself.

Christie didn't have time to hunt down another top, so he wiped off the edge of his goo-smeared cuff with a couple of baby wipes.

Missing Caro throbbed through him, feeling worse than the tooth that had needed a root canal last year. There were a thousand things he still wanted to do with her.

God. And that drunk who hit the car killing her and Liss was still around to do stuff with his family. It wasn't fair.

He squeezed Frankie into the slightly too small clothes. Her little Buddha belly peeping out at him stirred up memories of Liss rubbing Caro's pregnant belly. He swallowed the tightness in his throat and scooped up Frankie and the diaper bag. He grabbed his wallet and keys from where he'd thrown them on the kitchen counter the night before and they were headed to the car.

Christie buckled little Frankie into her car-seat, marveling at how much like her mother she looked, with her fair skin and bright blue eyes. She fought him every step of the way, wiggling, waving her little arms and even catching him on the chin with a well timed kick.

Caro, a little help here?

Caro? Hello, ghost girl, how is it you're able to be around to screw up every potential date I've run across lately, but not here when I need you?

"Geez Christie, you're a grouch this morning! Could you possibly think in a surlier tone of mind? No?"

Cut the crap Caro, and just work your magic.

"Fine, fine! Just be quiet and let me sing to her."

For Caro singing to the baby meant making up her own version of some lullaby. Today it was her special version of 'Hush little baby'.

Hush little Frankie

Don't say a word

Your Poppa's gonna buy you

A mockin' bird

An' if that mockin' bird don't sing

Momma's gonna put you in the baby-swing

An' if that baby-swing don't soothe

Momma's gonna sing an' get you in the groove...

The jazzy swing to the music calmed Frankie, her little body relaxing into the car seat and her eyelids getting droopy as her kicks slowed until they seemed to keep time with the music. After

Caro sang through it a few times, the baby was content with the bottle she was drinking from and the comforting presence of her favorite stuffed animal wedged in next to her as an impromptu pillow. Her little eyelids fell half shut.

Finally, they could get going. Christie closed her door quietly and then raced around to the driver's side. He blew out a frustrated breath as he slid behind the wheel.

Christ on a cracker. Frankie would know what Caro sounded like when she sang but she'd never really know *Caro*. She wouldn't know Liss either. Not as her moms.

Christie bit his top lip. If he got to post on time, and signed out on leave for the next month, he'd have time to get used to this slightly hollow and lopsided world without his best friend alive and sparkling in it somewhere, keeping it tilted at just the right angle.

Robert kept one eye on the scanner as he perused the morning's headlines. He couldn't believe they'd finally passed the LGBT Civil Rights Amendment. It tickled him to no end to know he now had as much right as anyone else to marry in the country that he spent every day keeping safe. He tipped his Sugar Creek to-go cup toward the paper as if toasting it. He thought about texting his youngest sister and asking her to pick up a couple extra copies of it…and then realized she would do that without any prompting from him. Nikki was a goddess, or at the very least a demigoddess. Robert had unabashedly worshipped at her feet since the day his mother brought her home from the hospital. Even when she was manipulating him into spending his entire annual vacation babysitting his niece for the second year in a row.

A silver car blew past him fast enough to rattle the pages of his paper through the open window. His scanner clocked the little Neon at seventy-two. Idiot. The speed limits were there to keep people safe.

Robert flipped his lights and siren on as he pulled onto the road.

The Neon quickly maneuvering to the shoulder of the road mollified him somewhat. He ran the car's plates through his computer, giving a cursory glance to ensure the driver had no outstanding warrants.

The car was registered in Gouveneur, NY to one Christie Collins, age twenty-six. Not reported stolen, no priors on the driver.

Robert unfolded himself from behind the wheel of his vehicle and placed his state trooper hat on his head. It was time to present Ms. Collins with the natural consequences of her actions. As he passed the rear of the car he saw a baby seat in the back of the car. Robert's temper spiked again. He rapped on the driver's side window, looking down as he finished filling out the handwritten portion of the idiot woman's ticket. The window whirred down, and then a faint sniffling sound came to his ears—if she thought a few tears were going to get her out of a justly deserved ticket she was dead wrong.

"Ms. Collins, I'm appalled that you would drive so far above the speed limit with an infant in your vehicle. I need your license, registration, and proof—"

The baby started wailing.

Robert knew he'd spoken sternly, but he hadn't intended it to be harsh enough to frighten the baby. The requested items were thrust at him even as she turned away toward the baby.

"I-I'm so-sorry officer. D-don't cry Frankie, it'll be okay. I promise it'll be o-okay honey. It's not the same as before. There w-wasn't an accident sweetie. Do you remember the flashing lights? I remember them too, baby. "

The voice wrapped around Robert as softly as the cashmere throws his Gran Olava used to put over him when he'd fallen asleep on her sofa. A warm heaviness invaded his groin.

Sweet Goddess, a woman was turning him on.

She had unbuckled her seat belt to twist her upper body thru the gap in the two front seats. In fact, she climbed half into the back seat, making shushing noises to her baby in between weepy sniffles and nonsensical babble. Her firm, round ass was in the air, wiggling back and forth until it ended up pointing straight at him as she bent over the driver's side seat. Robert's cock finished hardening in a rush. He whipped his trooper hat off to hold in front of his crotch.

"I-it's okay honey, don't cry. They can't fire me from the Army. And if the first sergeant takes my leave away for being late signing out I bet the daycare will let you come back e-early. Don't cry honey. I don't think they'll take you away b-because of o-one sp-speeding ticket…even if I can't pay it. I'll j-just get an article fifteen and…"

Robert felt about two inches tall. If she'd been in uniform he probably wouldn't have started writing the ticket, but it was too late now with the way everything was computerized and every printed ticket needing to be accounted for. He sighed. The least he could do for her was to give her a clear explanation of how she could get out of having to pay the fine. Hell, Judge Wallace was such a big supporter of the armed forces he'd probably completely wipe the ticket off her driving record.

"Look honey, I'm sorry you're late signing out on leave, but that's still no reason to speed, especially not with the precious cargo you're carrying. If you go to traffic court on the 17th, Judge Wallace has a rep for being extremely lenient with armed forces service members. Just explain to him what you were explaining to your baby there, and he'll most likely waive your ticket."

Robert walked back to his cruiser and printed the computerized section of the ticket off. After stapling it to the handwritten portion, he made sure to circle the part explaining how to contest the ticket. He highlighted the date and time of her court appearance. Satisfied he had done everything possible to help her, he walked back to stand next to her open window.

"Here's your ticket ma'am."

That got him a watery sounding chuckle. Robert looked up to assess whether she was becoming hysterical. What could end up being as much as a two hundred fifty dollar ticket, depending on the judge's ruling, was nothing to be laughing over. His gaze slid up from her lush pink mouth and honed in on mesmerizing blue-green eyes. He could easily imagine those gorgeous eyes looking up at him while the full lips were wrapped around his cock and all that sexy stubble…Robert's eyes flashed back to the stubble covered jaw.

Well.

Better than having to deal with finding himself suddenly bisexual at thirty-three years old. Robert knew he owed his dad a six pack of expensive German beer. It was stupid to bet against Robert Sr. when he started predicting how one of his kids would meet their 'special' someone. He'd told Robert he would fall in love at first sight.

Christie Collins. But he had a kid. No ring though…divorced? Widowed? Sweet Goddess, Robert hoped he was at least a little bent. It would be a waste if that man was completely straight.

Christie laughed nervously at the stunned expression on the handsome trooper's face. It wasn't the first time someone had taken a glance at him and mistaken him for a woman. It likely wouldn't be the last. He made a valiant attempt to corral his careening thoughts.

His laughter trailed away when the state trooper resettled his uniform hat on his head. The action revealed the prominent bulge the man was sporting. Christie nervously licked his lips.

The trooper had obviously seen something he liked while Christie was bent over leaning into the back seat. Christie hoped he didn't get angry about it now that he knew the person he'd gotten turned on by was a man.

"It's okay officer. I get that a lot. I hated my name when I was younger. I was gonna change it, cause there's already enough confusion over how I look. My mom really loved it though. I promised her I wouldn't change it before she died."

Christie glanced up at the trooper again. The flashing lights of his patrol car shone in the edges of Christie's vision. He gestured in their direction.

"She was killed in a car wreck. Drunk driver. That's why I hate the lights. Flashing. Umm, I won't change my name. That's what I meant. I keep it even though it causes me trouble sometimes. Once a guy didn't believe I was a man until I actually showed him the goods…er, sorry. That's probably not appropriate. I-I talk too much when I'm nervous. Umm. Could I have my ticket now? I really need to get to post."

The man, Trooper Lindstrom according to his name badge, gave Christie what looked like a half-lustful/half-incredulous look as he handed over the ticket. He then briskly popped his mirrored shades back on, silently tipped the round brim of his beige hat and strode back to his car. Christie watched the man's powerful looking thigh muscles bunch and release as he strode away.

After the trooper pulled out and around him, Christie sat for a few minutes, resting his hands on the steering wheel as he took slow, calming breaths. He tried biting his lip, but the pain wasn't enough to put him back together this time. He let his mind wander to the gorgeous trooper who had just screwed any chance he had of getting to the base before 0900.

Christie must have mistaken that look.

It couldn't have been lust.

The gorgeous trooper was probably straight.

What a waste.

Christ on a cracker, he'd even tried to be nice about the whole thing.

Christie refastened his seat belt, put his car in gear, and eased back onto the black top. He held his speed down the whole way to the base, carefully staying at least four miles below the speed limit the whole way. There was no way he could handle being pulled over again.

Christie had seen what they did to Jackson after his wife left him. The one time the guy got drunk and passed out on his own patio, his bitch of a neighbor called his command. Those bastards put his kids in foster care, saying he was neglectful and he had to wait until he got done with his enlistment to get them back. People just didn't get it.

It was hard enough to have a family in the military with two parents in the family, and only one a soldier. It was a hundred times harder when the one parent is the soldier. If they said Jackson was neglectful for falling asleep after a few beers—with his kids already in bed asleep—Christie could just imagine what would happen to him for speeding with Frankie in the car.

Shit.

He couldn't think about that without losing it again. Instead he'd just think about Trooper Hardbody. That was worthy of at least a little smile.

It was too bad all that gorgeous hot maleness was probably two dates away from a wedding with some girl. Christie glanced in the rearview mirror, smiling when he saw Frankie was contentedly sucking on two of her little fingers.

"Well, my little mouse, it's not like I could really have asked him out while he was writing my ticket anyway. He might have thought I was trying to bribe him with my luscious self."

Frankie pulled her fingers out of her mouth and smiled at him. He didn't care if the lady in the grocery store last week had told him that it was only gas. He knew better. His girl was laughingly agreeing with her poppa. She was a smart girl after all. Blowing spit bubbles, slobbering food all over yourself, and wetting your pants didn't become a sign of mental deficiency until sometime after your third birthday.

Christie's smile was bittersweet. If not for Liss and Caro dying in such an untimely manner, he might have missed every one of those sweetly gummy smiles. Tears prickled at the edge of his eyes. Resolutely wiping the back of his hand across his eyes, Christie determined to live every moment as the gift it was. Caro and Liss had put so much off for later. When they had enough money saved they would do such and such. When the baby was old enough to remember, they'd travel. They hadn't gotten a later. It would be a fitting tribute to them to savor every moment he had with Frankie, and all the people in his life.

CHAPTER TWO

Robert had spent the rest of his shift and the better part of the following three weeks acquiring information about the man whose beauty had struck him speechless. Once he found out—through a judicious misuse of state resources—that Mr. Collins was indeed single, Robert turned to racking his brains to think of a way to ask Christie Collins out without losing his job and going to jail. If he just showed up at the man's home address the likelihood of going down as a stalker was ludicrously high. Plus, even if Christie didn't press charges, it was creepy. Wait. It wasn't stalking if he didn't intend the person he was…investigating… any harm.

Oh shit.

He was a crazy stalker. It was bad enough skulking around looking for information on Christie…but to let Sergeant Byers cousin who worked as a secretary at post headquarters out of a speeding ticket for information from Christie's personnel packet?

Jeez.

That was stooping pretty low. If Robert couldn't figure out some way to get acquainted with Christie on the up and up, he was going to end up having to arrest himself for being creepy, among other things.

Robert's mind flashed to the last movie he'd watched with his niece Alyssa. He was still chuckling over the line the chief of police bear said about not being able to arrest someone just for being creepy when he finished up his paperwork for the current shift and started to head out in his civilian clothes.

"Lindstrom, come here a moment." Robert stopped at the sound of his captain's voice, backtracking to the office he'd just passed.

The older man started speaking before Robert got fully into the room. "Sergeant Byers just put in a request for family medical leave starting on the 17th, which leaves me short a man at the civil court from that night until the end of the month. Would you be willing to pick up a little overtime?"

Thank you, Goddess. He could stop looking for a way to accidently run into Mr. Collins.

"Sure Captain, I can work over. I've got the early shift that day, so I'd still have time to put on a fresh uniform and get to the court building before Judge Wallace gets there."

The captain gave Robert his look; the one that asked what sort of shenanigans you thought you were getting up to. Robert smirked back at the captain. He hoped when he'd been on the force for twenty some years, he'd be as savvy and compassionate as his captain.

"Hal Byers has covered shifts for me before, and it's a damned shame about his wife. Anything I can do to help him out, I will."

"Good man, Lindstrom."

Robert knew he'd been dismissed. He turned around and headed out the door, whistling to himself. He couldn't have asked for a sweeter set-up.

Four and a half weeks after Christie had what he considered the second most embarrassing incident of his life, he pulled into the parking lot of the county's traffic court. He was exhausted from the tough day he'd finished. Sergeant Rogers had been a total dick to him almost the entire time Christie had spent qualifying at the range. The non-commissioned officer running the range kept giving Christie every shit job there was to do until he finally realized Christie was putting three or more bullets into holes he'd already shot through his targets instead of missing his targets completely. Unfortunately, that didn't happen until after Christie survived hours and hours of being treated like a piece of crap Sergeant Rogers had found stuck to his favorite pair of combat boots. If he'd bothered to look at Christie's stats before accusing him of shooting into other people's targets, Sergeant Rogers would've realized Christie had never shot less than expert. Prick.

Christie let out a deep breath. He was still slightly off from his trip to bring Frankie to meet her grandparents. The home Caro had grown up in had reeked of loss. Even Frankie's joyous baby laughter hadn't been able to entirely dispel the gloom.

Her parents hadn't managed to reconcile with Caro before her death. It had taken Caro's death to shake them out of their rigid belief of what a family ought to be. They hadn't known Caro had a daughter until after Christie contacted them.

They would have tried to patch things up to be able to be part of their granddaughter's life. They still had all Caro's trophies from high school on the mantle of their fireplace collecting dust.

Christie was past sick of stupid drunks ripping his life apart.

He thought of how good it would feel to go back and find the stupid punk and beat him to a bloody heap on the ground. It wouldn't bring Liss and Caro back though. Nothing would.

Christie swung his little grey Neon into the parking lot of the local courthouse. The very empty parking lot seemed to mock him. The only non-official car in the lot was the one he was driving. Well, there was a big pick-up on the other side of the lot, but it was parked in the employee area, so Christie classified it as official in his mind.

Did he get the day wrong?

Shit.

After all the hassle his buddy Evans went through to keep him out of hot water on the day he'd gotten the damn ticket—

Christie shuddered. He had no idea how Evans had forced himself to go out with the beastly staff sergeant who'd been on duty—Crystal? Karen?—hell, whatever her name was, Evans had to lay the charm on pretty thick to get her to let Christie sign out with an earlier time.

She was still chasing after Evans.

Christie owed his buddy big time for putting up with that to keep him off First Sergeant Bartone's radar. If he'd screwed it up by missing his court date, Evans was gonna rip him a new one.

Christie double checked the date on the ticket he'd stashed in his glove box. Today was the 17th. It was exactly 1915. The ticket boldly proclaimed 7:30pm as the time he was supposed to be here, so he was actually fifteen minutes early. Heh. Good Army training at work there. So where was everyone?

Putting the car into park, Christie peered through the windshield. There was something taped to the door of the squat little building that housed the county's traffic court. He got out of the car and walked close enough to read the rough scrawl on the paper that was taped to the stout wooden door.

"Court cancelled today due to illness. You are hereby directed to return at 5:30pm on the 27th of this month for your court appointment." Crap. He'd been back from leave for a few days and it was sheer luck he'd had an early dismissal time today. They were released early for beating Third Platoon in the obstacle course competition. Tonight's turn of events meant he'd have to tell his squad leader he had to appear in court, or risk getting caught in a lie. Shit. It just figured. Christie stared at the damning little scrap of paper. He'd really wanted to keep his chain of command in the dark about this one.

"Judge Wallace called in sick at the last minute. He almost never gets sick though, so it's a good bet he'll actually be here on the 27th."

Christie gave an embarrassingly girly little squeak as he whirled around, hand on his chest. His humiliation was complete. The sneaky creeper was none other than Trooper Hot Body—er—Lindstrom. He squeezed his eyes shut and prayed for the ground to open and swallow him up. No dice. It stayed distressingly firm beneath his feet. He cracked one eye open. Yep. Trooper Lick-a-licious, the star of every pornographic fantasy he'd jacked off to since receiving the most expensive ticket in the history of mankind was still standing there.

The trooper had an openly amused expression on his face. That made sense. It seemed like every time Christie was within five hundred yards of the man he lost all ability to function as a rational adult.

"Ah…Trooper Lindstrom, h-how are you this evening?" A blush flooded across his caramel skin.

Christ on a cracker, could he possibly sound any more idiotic?

"I'm doing rather well, Mr. Collins. You're actually the last one to show up of the defendants scheduled to appear tonight. So now that I'm assured you've received the information regarding when your appearance has been rescheduled for, I'm off duty."

The man gave Christie an arch look, one eyebrow raised, his cerulean eyes gleaming with lust. The darkening eyes, coupled with his flaring nostrils and the growing bulge in his uniform pants told the tale. Either the man was turned on by the idea of a judge calling in sick (unlikely), or he was doing his damndest to salute Christie in the very best way (hopefully).

At that moment Frankie—bless her discerning little heart— gave an enormous wail. Phew! He was saved by the bell before he lost his mind and climbed Trooper Hot-body like a challenge trail.

"Um. Yes. Th-thank you, trooper. I have to go."

Now, before he embarrassed himself more.

Christie all but sprinted for his car. He needed to escape before Trooper Lindstrom classified him at the extreme end of the spasmodic spectrum. The very last thing he needed was someone in a position of power questioning his mental fitness.

Christie remembered watching his Aunt Cate being treated like she was ever so slightly mentally deficient by the very same men whose department had called for her assistance in one 'impossible' case after another. Their excuse for being rude was simply that she claimed to talk to ghosts. He couldn't ever let anyone in his chain of command find out about Caro. Then they'd take Frankie away for sure and give him a one-way ticket to the huggie-jacket farm.

He scrambled into the driver's seat. As he fumbled with his seat belt, he glanced up and found Trooper Lindstrom at his window. Christie rolled it down hesitantly.

"Was there something else?"

"Yes. I wanted to know if you'd like to have dinner with me tonight."

Christie gaped at the man. He blinked a few times, trying to rearrange his mental image of who this man was. It didn't work. "I thought you were straight!"

The tall golden haired man laughed. Christie was fairly sure there had to be a law somewhere against being that good-looking and charismatic to boot. The trooper's grin tilted up on one side.

"Straight? Not so much."

It was a nice laugh, warm and sort of chuckly.

A fretful whimper emanated from the backseat. Saved by the baby. The last thing Christie needed was to melt into a gooey puddle in front of the sexy state trooper.

"I'd love to have dinner with you, but I have to get my daughter home. It's past her bedtime. And she still needs to eat. Um."

Christie desperately clamped his lips together to stem the cascade of babble. He'd probably ruined any chance he had with the sexy state trooper. About two days after Frankie came to live with him he'd come to the depressing conclusion that while suddenly being a single guy with a baby might be a dream come true for a straight guy's sex/love life, it was the kiss of death for a gay man.

He'd had about a zillion horny women sidle up to him in those first two days alone...it was unfortunate the fairer sex did absolutely nothing for him sexually. To make matters worse, at the same time, every potentially hot/obviously gay man he'd seen had pretty much run screaming for the hills.

Christie figured they must have mistaken him for a married closet case, or, worse yet, an actual straight man. Unless he just wanted random hookups in the seedy back rooms of the few gay friendly bars that were local, he was pretty much doomed to not having sex with anyone but himself for the next eighteen or twenty years. He was a lot more sympathetic to the bitchy attitude of some of the single moms in his unit now. It was tough to have a good attitude when you hadn't gotten any for a while, and weren't going to get any in the foreseeable future.

"Well, I hope I'm not being too forward, but could we cook at your place then?"

Holy. Mother. Of. God. Trooper Lindstrom wasn't running for the hills with a terrified expression.

"He likes you. He wants to date you. Kiss you and hold you."

A smirk crept across Christie's face. Caro used to chant that in his ear whenever a guy showed interest in him. It figured she'd find a way to keep doing it after death. He let his expression mellow into a genuine smile.

"I'd like that. You can follow me to my place…um…what's your first name? I'll feel a little funny calling you Trooper Lindstrom over dinner."

That incandescent smile appeared again.

"Robert. My name is Robert. If you keep calling me Trooper Lindstrom over dinner I'll be tempted to break my cuffs out to see how they'll look on you."

A zing of electricity shot through Christie. Breathing suddenly seemed a task suited only to Nobel Prize winners. The temperature jumped up a good ten degrees, and he found he had to flare his nostrils to pull in the slightest hint of fresh air.

"Oh. Then perhaps I should call you Trooper Lindstrom all the time."

The blue of Robert's eyes darkened even more as Christie watched. The man's cheekbones were rapidly covered with a hectic flush of color as well. Christie really, really liked the notion of being vulnerable to this particular man's whims.

"What do you want for dinner Christie? I'll stop at the grocery and pick it up while you feed your daughter and get her put to bed."

Oh. That was nice. The offer gave Christie a sense of being looked after caringly. This must be what it felt like to have a partner to share the responsibilities and tasks of parenthood with. Christie wanted that so much. Sometimes as he sat alone in the house after he put Frankie to bed the longing to have someone to curl up and simply be with would suddenly sweep over him. Some nights it was so fierce his jaws would ache from clenching them against the loneliness. And Christ on a cracker, if his jaws had to ache, Christie could certainly think of much more fun ways to make that happen.

"A couple of steaks would be nice, and some salad. If you wouldn't mind picking up some Good Start formula, that would be a life-saver. Frankie uses the one with the yellow label."

Christie reached into his jacket pocket to pull out his wallet. Robert reached in through the window to put a hand on his arm. Glancing up in surprise, Christie saw that the man was shaking his head no.

"I've got this one Christie. You go get your daughter taken care of and I'll meet you at your house in about thirty minutes. You're at 1137 Larch Circle right? Do you like wine? If you do I'll pick up a bottle of that as well."

He likes you. He wants to date you. Kiss you and hold you.

Christie ignored Caro in favor of gazing up at the man, perplexed as to how he knew the address. He'd seemed so perfect, dammit! Now, with that easy rattling off of Christie's address, the big man was edging a little towards the scary end of the spectrum. Swallowing nervously Christie tried to come up with a quick yet diplomatic way to bow out of the last minute date.

Robert must have seen some of Christie's unease reflected in his face.

"Your address was on the ticket I wrote, remember? I have a really good memory for that kind of stuff. It's part of why I went into law enforcement."

Robert saw the relief flow over Christie, visibly relaxing the muscles his idiotic blurting had drawn taut. Jeez, he'd almost blown it. He wanted to know how Christie had come to have a daughter, because everything about the smaller man screamed out his unabashed gayness. He wanted to know what made him laugh, what made him angry, and most especially what Christie looked like stretched out across a bed, his hands cuffed above his head.

"I—how? I mean okay. Okay. Um. Yes, I like wine. I especially like Dancing Bull's 2007 merlot. It's my favorite. Um...I'll see you in a little while?"

Straightening up, Robert allowed himself to run one finger along the side of Christie's face. He forced himself to stop shy of the plush bottom lip that seemed to cry out for his touch. He knew once he touched it the last shred of his self control would evaporate. He didn't want that to happen until they were somewhere private.

"Yeah Christie...you'll see me in just a little while. You said your daughter takes the Good Start that has a yellow label?"

"That's right."

Robert found himself pulled forward by the breathless quality of Christie's reply. He started to bend down to kiss the man before stopping himself. Christie's presence had already tested his willpower too far. He stopped and backed away toward his truck.

"Since I'm going to get the wine too, give me between thirty and forty-five minutes to pick the stuff up and get to your house."

"Okay."

Robert forced himself to turn around and walk around the front of his truck. If he hustled he'd have enough time to stop at the pharmacy for some lube and condoms. He didn't know if anything was going to happen tonight, but it never hurt to be prepared. He started up his truck and drove thoughtfully in the opposite direction of the disappearing silver Neon. He'd found the man meant for him and a way to start dating him which didn't involve lawsuits or being convicted of stalking. It felt pretty damned good. He was just glad to have a little bit of time to wrap his head around it. Robert reached into his console, pulling out his thick silver bracelet. He slid it on thinking it couldn't hurt to have one more thing to ground him.

CHAPTER THREE

As soon as he got in the door, Christie grabbed a pre-made bottle of formula out of the refrigerator and stuck it in the sink under the hot water. It would warm up in about five minutes. In the mean time he could pop Frankie in her bouncy seat and he would have just enough time to throw some charcoal in the grill and get it lighted. The coals would be perfect by the time Robert got here.

"He likes you. He wants to date you. Kiss you and hold you."

"Shut up, Caro! Christ on a cracker woman, ghosts are supposed to bump stuff around and show up as vague misty outlines that scare the crap out of people, not chant silly teases out in people's brains and sing their kids to sleep."

As soon as the words left his mouth Christie wished them unsaid. It was petty to begrudge Caro what interaction she could have with Frankie and him. He just really wanted Robert to like him. Christie knew if Caro kept teasing him he might slip up and talk to her out loud. Then the man would think Christie needed a trip to the local psych ward. He didn't even know if E.J. Noble Hospital had a psych ward. They might have to transport him all the way down to Syracuse, and that would be bad. It—he was rambling. He took a deep breath to calm down.

"I'm sorry Caro. Just please, please tone it down tonight, okay? I like this guy. There's something about him Caro. Please don't make him think I'm crazy. Or that he's crazy. I…I'm lonely. I miss you and Liss. I miss being able to date casually. Now it's deadly serious right from the start. I promised I'd never let Frankie have a slew of pseudo uncles. Just—please help me not screw this up!"

A cool touch whispered across Christie's cheek. A faint patchouli scent hung in the air. He was forgiven. If she was still mad the smell would be Obsession. He'd always hated that perfume on her. Whether Caro planned to help him appear worth a second date remained to be seen, but at least she wouldn't be deliberately sabotaging his attempts.

He took a moment to check Miss Kitty's food and water bowls. Both dishes were nearly empty, so he topped them off. Now that Caro had vacated the room, Miss Kitty would be making an appearance. Christie wished he could get a straight answer out of Caro about why the two of them seemed to always avoid each other. Right now, it was one of those little mysteries that kept life from becoming monotonous.

Exactly forty-five minutes after parting company with Christie, Robert pulled up in the man's driveway for the first time. It was surreal to be getting ready to have dinner with the person he'd been having happily-ever-after dreams about for most of the last month. He'd described Christie's face numerous times in his dream journal. It—Robert shook his head. He had to back burner all that divination stuff for right now. He didn't want Christie to think he was some new age nut.

Robert had picked up two porterhouse steaks, a Caesar salad kit, and a bottle of 2007 Dancing Bull merlot. He had a new economy sized box of condoms and a pocket sized bottle of Astroglide in the truck as well.

Using his thumbnail, he quickly slit open the box of condoms and tore a strip of six off. He slid the small bottle of lube into his pocket along with the condoms. Then he gathered up the rest of his purchases and headed up the walk to ring Christie's doorbell.

Christie opened the door before Robert could step up to the bell. He must have been hovering in the hallway, waiting for it to ring. Christie put a finger to his lips.

"Ssshh. I just got her down. Come through to the kitchen before you say anything, okay?"

The feeling of Christie's warm breath on his ear caused a shudder to pass through Robert. He nodded his head in understanding. On silent feet he followed Christie through the house to the kitchen. Once there he set the bags down and Christie started pulling stuff out of them.

"You got porterhouse; I love these steaks."

Christie beamed at Robert, his sexy lips curved up and shining as he swept his tongue over them. The expression sucked all the air from Robert's lungs.

"And you found 2007 Dancing Bull."

Robert managed to continue to operate without oxygen. Anything to keep that expression on Christie's face.

"They didn't have the Good Start with the yellow label where I stopped, Christie. I thought I could run to the other grocery store after dinner to pick some up for you. The girl at the first store said they won't have any until Thursday."

Christie smiled at him again. Robert felt about twenty feet tall.

If this worked out, Christie was gonna find out pretty quickly that Robert would do just about anything to keep that look of delight on his face. Sweet Goddess, he made Robert feel like a superhero just for offering to pick up a can of baby formula.

Robert pulled his thoughts forcefully out of Christie's pants to pay attention to what he was saying. It was damn hard to do. The other man kept biting at his top lip and then soothing the spot with the tip of his tongue. Robert made his eyes rise from that spot to meet Christie's.

"It's really okay, Robert. I have enough stuff to get us through until Thursday, and I have to go shopping then anyway, so I'll pick some up when I go."

Robert's gaze drifted back to Christie's succulent mouth.

He really had to focus on something else.

He glanced through the living room, spotting a grill on the patio. Robert pulled the steaks out of Christie's hands.

"Did you want to grill them?"

Christie made an affirmative sounding noise. He swayed forward, a slightly glazed look appearing in his blue-green eyes. If he got any closer Robert was going to forget about dinner, throw the man's sexy little ass down on the nearest available flat surface, and fuck every bit of breath out of his tight body.

As much as he would like that, he really didn't know Christie well enough to go all cave-man.

Yet.

Though he could always hope to play that fantasy out later.

Robert forced himself to focus on the steaks. "I'll need some charcoal. Do you have any?"

Christie shook himself like a dog coming out of the water and blinked.

"Hmmmm? Oh, yeah, charcoal. It's already in the grill. I started it as soon as I got home. The coals should be almost ready."

Robert hastily retreated to the patio. There was a trash can against the wall of the house, so he put the packaging in there once he got the steaks on the grill. Christie followed him out a few minutes later with the salad in a big green and brown ceramic bowl, the wine, and two glasses. Setting it all down on the table he pulled a corkscrew out of his pants pocket and set it next to the wine. Then he held up the last item he'd been carrying. It was a bright blue full length apron. The slogan emblazoned on it in stylized white letters read: *Carl's Meat Market: Where Great Cooks get Rump and Tongue!!*

Robert sputtered for a moment before he gave in to the laughter struggling to escape from inside him. It looked like Christie had a great sense of humor. He liked that. He was still chuckling as he bent down to let the shorter man slip the neck strap over his head. He dutifully turned around so Christie could tie the apron strings at the back of his waist. Robert bit down on the desire to blurt out how right it felt to be with Christie like this. It was one thing to share the hopes springing from his nightly dreams about living happily ever after with Christie when he was talking with his family. They all believed in such things. It was something else entirely to blurt out that you thought someone was your soul-mate during a first date. He picked up the corkscrew, opened the wine, and poured a glass for Christie.

"Sit down Christie. You look beat. Just tell me where you keep the plates and silverware. I'll get everything."

Robert pushed the second barstool around from the far side of the tall table. He lifted Christie's feet up onto the seat, unlacing and pulling the man's boots off as he did. He listened carefully to the instructions of where to find the dishes and silverware. Then he topped off Christie's wine and went inside to fetch the last few things they needed for dinner.

When he came back outside he pulled the sliding screen all the way shut but left the glass slider cracked open. Looking up, he saw Christie canting his head to one side, an eyebrow raised in question.

"So you can hear the baby if she cries."

Christie wanted to pinch himself. He had to be dreaming. A hot guy who wanted to stay in with him, cooked for him, and insisted he put his feet up to rest. That only happened on cheesy sitcoms; in the ridiculous 'romance' novels he and Evans were so partial to…oh, and in dreams. This was a nice dream though, with the potential to become a nicely naughty dream, one he wasn't waking up from any sooner than he had to. If only he could come home to this every day.

"Who's Caro? You have post-its all over the side of those gorgeous bookshelves with notes about things you need to tell her."

The question hit like a full strength kick to the chest he'd failed to block. Okay, dream over. How did he explain Caro though? Or better yet, how did he dance around the edges of explaining Caro?

"She was my best friend, and Francesca's mom. She and her partner were killed in a car accident a little over two months ago. Because I'm the other biological parent, I got Frankie."

Robert looked mortified. Christie hadn't meant to make

the man feel bad. He was sure it was supposed to get easier at some point to say that Caro and Liss were gone. He just had no idea when that time would come, or how to talk about it in the meantime without making everyone around him feel awkward.

Christie set his glass down.

"Oh, don't look like that. There was no way for you to know. I-I know I should take the notes down. I just...it makes it too real if I do that."

Christie covered his eyes. His cheeks flooded with heat as embarrassment swept over him. It would be easier not to see Robert leaving.

"I—um, don't think I'm crazy please, okay? I even still write new ones. When Frankie does something new, you know? Something Caro would have wanted to see."

None of the other dates he'd had stuck around this long.

"I-it's okay. I'll drop some cash off at the trooper barracks to pay you back for the food. I'm sorry."

Robert didn't say anything. Christie heard footsteps. He bit down on his lip, trying to hold his tears back until the sound of the slider screen closing let him know the man was gone, his eyes squeezed shut.

He was so damned tired of wanting to punch something or bursting into tears like a sniveling child.

Shit. He missed his Tae-Kwon Do classes. They at least let him work off some steam. He really needed to find a reliable babysitter.

Christie was suddenly lifted up out of his chair. His eyes flew open to find himself in the process of being cradled against Robert's broad chest. The larger man sat in the chair he'd just plucked Christie out of. He settled Christie in his lap, gently stroking his back. When he spoke, his voice was thick with his own ghosts.

"I lost my best friend in a car accident. I couldn't even say his name for a whole year afterwards. I didn't cry. I didn't sleep.

I barely ate. Finally my Gran made me sit on her lap in her old rocker. I was as tall as I am now, and Gran is only five-three. I'm sure we looked a sight. She just held me there, and rocked, and said his name over and over and over until I cried. We must have rocked for two hours like that, me crying, Gran rubbing my back and telling Cody goodbye for me."

Christie's reply came out scarcely louder than a whisper.

"You understand."

Robert's arms tightened around him as the bigger man spoke.

"I do."

They sat like that until the tantalizing scent of meat cooking over hot coals wafted over them. Robert stood up, turned, and placed Christie back in his seat, kissing him gently on the temple. Then he topped off Christie's glass handing it to him nearly full.

"Drink a little of that while I finish up these steaks."

Christie blinked, willing his stupid eyes to stop watering. He was sick of looking like an idiot or a preadolescent girl in front of this man. It couldn't be a beautiful dream if he cried all the way through it. Robert's voice pulled him out of his thoughts.

"It's okay to cry for your friend. Once Gran got me to cry I cried at the drop of a hat for the next eight months. It…it's an honor for your friend, as it was for Cody. I believe it shows that they were worthy of love."

Robert paused there, looking like he was choosing his words very carefully.

"That's what you were really crying about wasn't it? The first time we met?"

Robert had snuck that question in as he slid the steaks onto the platter. It was a pretty slick move, but Christie wasn't falling for it. He decided to deflect the question rather than answer it.

"Damn. Good looking, smart, and a good cook. Why aren't you married?"

Robert locked eyes with him, his lips curving up slightly at the corners. "I guess I never met the right man. And it wasn't legal everywhere in the US until about four and a half weeks ago."

Christie caught his breath. Robert kept right on looking at him, and suddenly Christie was thinking maybe Robert thought he'd finally met the right one. The air thickened between them. Christie continued to stare into Robert's eyes until the other man placed the platter on the table, and the loud clink of the ceramic dish against the glass of the table-top caused him to blink. Robert smiled again as he lifted Christie's feet to slip into the chair closest to him.

"The steaks are ready, beautiful. Let's eat."

CHAPTER FOUR

Robert hated to see Christie cry. He tried to plot a better course for the rest of their evening while he ate. One that didn't include the blunders he'd made so far.

The beautiful man currently wolfing down his steak like he hadn't eaten in days was definitely going to be his. It might not happen tonight, and it might be a while before he could tell Christie he wanted to keep him forever without sounding like a nut, but it was going to happen.

Christie smiled at him.

"This is good. I usually overcook mine lately because I get distracted by the baby. I could get used to having decently cooked steak."

"Well, I could get used to cooking it for you." Goddess. That was pure shmultz. His brain must have short circuited from the sight of Christie's smile.

Robert squeezed his eyes shut. It was amazing that he had ever managed to get anyone to go on a second date with him. Maybe it was just with Christie he became such a knuckle dragger.

"Uh. If you wanted me to, that is."

Yeah. That wasn't awkward. Now he sounded like he was skating right on the edge of creepy pushiness. At this rate, he'd do better to staple his mouth shut.

He closed his mouth so nothing else stupid could escape out of it. He cracked his eyes back open and cast a cursory glance over Christie's plate. It was more or less empty. Good. There was only one way to salvage this. He leaned over and kissed Christie.

Best. Dream. Ever. It had to be. Christie didn't think this could possibly be happening to him in real life. Robert tasted spicy, like A-1 steak sauce, Caesar dressing, and something that was just him. Bold, warm, and exhilarating; the flavor made Christie shake just a little. He could spend hours tasting this man.

Lack of oxygen finally forced him to remove his mouth from Robert's. Christie blinked as he registered his tight grip on the larger man's shoulders, and the firm, burning heat of Robert's waist against his wrapped legs. He was doing a damned fine impression of a horny spider-monkey by clinging to Robert while grinding his rampant erection against the sexy trooper's rock hard abs.

"How'd I get up here? When did you stand up?"

He must have sounded as bewildered as he felt. Robert was suddenly laughing so hard, the man could barely stand. The big trooper leaned against the side of the house right next to the sliding glass doors and brought their mouths back together.

Christie was pretty sure Robert's tongue was trying to teach his the Paso Doble or some equally intricate and intense Latin dance. He writhed against Robert, their chests rubbing against one another. Christie moaned into Robert's mouth. He slid his lips up along Robert's jaw and quietly growled out a request directly into Robert's ear. He was supremely conscious of the fact that too much noise would wake Frankie, calling a halt to all the adult fun currently going on.

"Inside." Christie's low growl reverberated against Robert's firm chest. "Get inside. Naked. Get naked inside."

Robert peeled Christie off his front and then pried the smaller man's legs from around his waist. He set Christie down on his own feet. The man grinned like some cheesy cartoon character the whole time. He reached behind himself and pulled the sliders open. "Now there's a plan I'm all for getting behind, Christie."

Then his lips were where they belonged, back on Christie's, and they were stumbling through the living room and into the bedroom. Robert paused then, his face serious and tender. He cupped Christie's cheek in one big hand.

"Christie, are you sure about this? I don't mind waiting…well, that's a lie, I would mind, but I'll wait if you need more time. I don't want to take advantage."

Christie grabbed the edges of Robert's borrowed apron. Growling, he used it to swing the larger man around. Once he had his yummy trooper positioned, he shoved with all his strength. Robert fell back on the big antique German bed. He looked like a smorgasbord of hot Nordic fuckableness.

"Oh, hell no, Robert. Take advantage of me as many times as you want."

Robert chuckled and started getting naked. He found it a little hard to concentrate on what he was doing though. Christie had pulled his brown uniform t-shirt over his head. Robert started to sit up, hands reaching for all that silky looking skin.

Christie danced back out of reach, his face stern.

"Naked, Robert. Now."

Robert snorted with laughter. He was willing to bet the man in front of him had no idea how sexy Robert found it when he spoke that way. Christie's demanding speech made heat flash up Robert's spine. He flopped back down, unbuckled his belt, and started pushing his gray uniform pants past his hips. Hands pulled at his ankles, tugging the pants down and then off. He was surprised to see that Christie had gotten completely undressed before helping him with his pants. Another shot of heat rushed up his spine.

Christie swarmed up Robert's body, not stopping until he was stretched full length over the larger man with their groins perfectly lined up. With his head turned down to press kisses along Robert's collar bone and upper chest it was impossible to see what, if anything, he was feeling beyond pure lust. The kisses were hot, openmouthed things one moment, full of teeth and fire, and then they would slow to languid, almost reluctantly tender explorations. Robert wondered if Christie even realized how his alternating-current kisses were showing that this was more than just physical, that he was feeling the same soul deep pull of attraction as Robert.

Then Christie lifted his hips just enough to slide a hand between their bodies. It was as if Robert were a never-been touched virgin as Christie's strong, lean hand wrapped partially around both their cocks. Knowing what Christie could mean to him, changed everything for Robert, and made it all seem brand new.

Christie's hand began to stroke impatiently up and down. He kept shifting and making frustrated grunting noises. The angle Christie had looked wrong; not enough traction or balance to make everything work how he wanted it to.

"A little help here, Robert?"

Robert smiled. Christie made his heart feel light. They weren't on the same page yet, but for this man he could be patient. He slid his hands slowly along the skin of Christie's sides and back. It was just as silky as it looked. Christie was braced up on one arm. He glared at Robert.

"Bossy little bottom, aren't you Christie?"

Robert slid a hand between them to join Christie's in wrapping around their cocks. They both hissed in pleasure when he tangled his fingers with Christie's and pulled their joined hands up and down the length of their shafts. A pulse of connection seeped into him from those intertwined fingers, running straight into his heart. Robert loved the feeling.

Christie met Robert's gaze squarely.

"Yes I am. I'm bossy, and I'm a bottom. That okay with you?"

"Oh, hell yeah."

Robert loved the forceful way Christie stated his preferences. He loved…he forced the first thing he wanted to say back behind his teeth. A little patience now would give Christie a chance to catch up without feeling rushed or pressured.

Robert's fingers took a slow journey along Christie's hips to meet in the center of his back at the dip just above the swell of his rounded cheeks. He smiled and lifted the man's delicious body off his own. He wiggled over to the edge of the bed and pulled the strip of condoms and the travel bottle of Astroglide out of his pants pocket. He turned back around to find Christie giving him an indecipherable look.

"Huh. Guess you were pretty sure you were getting laid tonight." Christie arched an eyebrow at Robert.

As those words sank in, Robert took his turn at blushing. Damn. Christie had gotten the wrong impression.

"Actually I was pretty sure I wasn't. I just didn't want to take the chance that we might get here and not have any protection. I couldn't stand to leave you hanging, and I'd never put you at risk."

Robert said too much.

Christie was his perfect mate; his forever. That didn't mean Christie knew it yet. His nerves spun a little tighter as the smaller man watched him silently.

He likes you. He wants to date you. Fuck and fellate you.

Christ on a cracker, this was so not the appropriate time for Caro to be popping in. The big gorgeous trooper was talking like they were already a well established couple and Christie needed to decide what he wanted to do about that. He squeezed his eyes shut to concentrate on talking to Caro.

"*Dammit Caro, get the hell out of here! I've got all my junk hanging out, I'm trying to figure out how I feel about his level of preparedness, his assumptions about there being an* us, *and as much as I want to get on the super-sexy-trooper ride, I don't want* you *watching him fuck and fellate me."*

Christie figured he'd get around to discussing how his dead friend haunted him on his second or two thousandth date with Robert. If the big nutball's behavior could be overlooked enough to get him to a second date. Robert was watching him intently with a sweetly anxious expression on his Viking-god face.

"Christ on a cracker, Robert. The things you say. I can't argue with it being good planning to have supplies handy in case we ended up needing them. And since you weren't expecting anything, just hoping…. Better glove up and get your curveballs all greased up. Although perhaps in your case I should say curved bat?"

Christie laughed playfully as he stroked Robert's crooked shaft to be sure the other man knew just what he was teasing him about. He wanted to make sure his sexy trooper knew it was light-hearted.

"Well, Mr. Collins, if you're going to start making comments about the pitcher's equipment I guess you'd better call me Trooper Lindstrom so I feel comfortable cuffing you and performing a cavity search."

Christie loved how the little lilt of laughter snuck into Robert's rich baritone as he spoke. Robert was looking down at where Christie's hand still curled lightly around the trooper's rock hard cock. Tonight he needed something different though. He let go of Robert's pulsating shaft and curled his hand under the other man's chin. He turned Robert's face up so they were looking one another in the eye.

"I'd love to play that game another night. Tonight can we just be you and me, Robert and Christie, the state trooper and the soldier?"

Robert smiled a soft, sweet smile and nodded his head. "I can do that."

Christie watched as Robert grabbed up the strip of condoms, tore one off, opened it, and efficiently rolled a condom down his length, checking to ensure it fit snugly at the base of his cock. The man carefully slathered a fair amount of lubricant over the condom then looked up. The movement of his strong hand along his cock mesmerized Christie. The small muscles and prominent tendons stood out on the back of his hand as he stroked up and down a few times, clearly enjoying the sensation. Robert's hand and cock both glistened in the low light of the bedside lamp. Christie couldn't help wishing it was flavored lube so he could get a big mouthful of Robert's shaft and suck like it was a tootsie-roll pop he was hunting for the center of.

"Has it been very long Christie? I want in you right now, but I wanna make sure you have enough prep."

"You are so damned sexy and sweet. You can go straight in Robert, as long as you take it slow. I open up easy."

Robert looked toward the ceiling. His lips moved without sound.

"Robert…what are you saying?"

Locking eyes with Christie again, the trooper smiled. He lifted a hand from his well lubed cock and reached between Christie's legs. He trailed one slippery finger between the smaller man's silk-smooth buttocks, teasing around his puckered opening. His heat ghosted over the sensitive skin.

"I was thanking all the gods that you exist."

Robert slid one long finger slowly into Christie.

"Get on your back, Christie. I want to watch your face when I push you over the edge."

Christie eased onto his back, his eyes fluttered closed at that stretch. It was good, but…

"More, Robert."

Robert's finger was joined by another. The hot, slick digits seemed to stroke straight along Christie's spine, deep enough to steal the air from his lungs.

It had been a while since Christie had a lover; there was a slight sting to that deep, pressing stroke. Christie rocked his hips up toward the invading fingers, craving the burn.

Robert slid those fingers carefully in and out. He crooked them up and white hot heat shot up Christie's spine.

It wasn't enough.

"Give me more, Robert. Now."

The fingers stilled inside him.

"Bossy."

Christie grinned.

"Never denied it. Are you satisfied yet?"

Robert maneuvered himself between Christie's widespread legs.

"Not even close, Christie."

CHAPTER FIVE

Robert slung one of Christie's legs up over his broad, muscular shoulder. He quirked an eyebrow at the man under him, and as clearly as if he'd spoken, Christie knew just what he was asking.

"I can do a full split. Twelve years of Tae-Kwon-Do. I'm like Christie-Gumby at this point. Just put my legs wherever you want them."

It appeared that where Robert wanted them was damn near a split at first. The stretch in his thighs added to the mass of pleasurable sensations bombarding Christie. Robert lined the head of his condom covered cock up with Christie's hole and pressed forward. The muscular ring guarding Christie's anal entrance melted open. Slowly, steadily, Robert kept the pressure even until he popped through. A raw sound escaped him then. It was a cross between a groan and a growl, and so damned sexy Christie almost came right then. His balls tingled as they pulled up tight to his body. He grabbed the base of his cock and used his fingers to make an impromptu cock ring.

"You feel so tight babe…are…you. Christie…you. Sure. I'm not. Hurting you?"

Christie smiled. He pulled Robert's face down to his and gave him a long, deep kiss while he brought one of Robert's hands to his granite hard cock.

"Cocks don't lie, Robert. What does this tell you?"

Robert smiled. He let his back sway. Gravity did the rest, and his cock slowly, deliciously sank into Christie's hungry ass.

"That steely cock tells me you're enjoying yourself, and right now you need a good hard pounding."

Christie smiled, tapping the end of his nose. Then Robert did something weird with his hips, a swivel and a twist at the same time. The beautiful, god blessed, bent tip of his cock tapped against Christie's prostate. Once, twice, and Christie was coming like he'd never come before, white coating the edges of his vision while black spots danced across the center. It was shockingly fast, and if Christie wasn't still twitching with aftershocks he might have been able to dredge up the wherewithal to feel something besides fucked stupid.

Robert asked, "You did open up like a dream, but it's been a while hasn't it sweet baby?"

Christie let his head flop forward in an approximation of a nod. He was blissfully incapable of speech at the moment.

Robert pulled his hips back slowly, repeating the same maddening sequence of thrust, twist, and tap.

"You're going to be mine, Christie."

Robert's husky growl reverberated against the sparks still igniting inside Christie.

"We can take the dating as slow as you want. I just want you to know that you're going to be mine forever."

"He wants to keep you… don't let it slip past you, Christie. I didn't tell Liss I loved her the day we died, and now I can't find her. Grab your chance with both hands sweetie."

Robert froze for a second. Then he slipped back into the same wonderful rhythm as before, Robert's chin was firmed up, his lips pressed into a no-nonsense line. His eyes held a wistful yearning in their cerulean depths. He'd never had anyone look at him quite like that before. Robert's hips kept pumping away, the speed gradually increasing. Christie watched him, feeling thoughtful rather than frightened by his declaration.

"Okay. But I reserve the right to change my mind."

Christie squeezed his eyes shut. This was still the best dream ever. He didn't ever want to wake up. He just needed to get Caro out of his head for right now.

Shut up Caro. And get out of my bedroom. Go sing to Frankie.

For once, Caro did exactly as he asked without arguing. He and Robert would have plenty of time to share secrets as they got to know each other. He whispered to Robert lovingly, saying the words he knew his new man was waiting to hear.

"Let go, lover. Let go. I'm here to catch you."

Robert let go, and damned if the man didn't manage to bring Christie right along with him. The feel of Robert's crooked cock tapping on his prostate as the man shuddered through his orgasm combined with the scorching, intense look in his cerulean eyes surprised Christie into another climax. They ended up catching each other. Christie drifted in a post-orgasmic haze, Caro's singing drifting gently in from the other room. Robert muttered against his neck.

"Smart Christie, so clever...leaving the radio on for the baby...bet...helps her...sleep."

Christie wiggled out from under the exhausted man falling asleep on him. He grabbed a couple of washcloths from the bathroom after he washed up and tended to Robert; rousing him just enough to find out what time the troopers were expecting him in the morning. It turned out they weren't expecting him tomorrow at all. It was his day off. Christie cuddled into Robert's side, pulled the comforter up over them both, and let Caro's song lull him to sleep.

"He wants to love you, kiss you and hold you."

Christie eyed the crowds thronging the local farmer's market. A heavy feeling settled into his stomach. Shit. He hated fighting for parking spaces. He hoped the parking lot Robert had given him directions to would have an open spot when he got there.

Robert had insisted that meeting here would be fun. As Christie whipped his little car into a spot just vacated by a big pickup truck he grimaced. Christ on a cracker, if this was Robert's idea of a ripping good time they might not be as compatible as Christie had thought during their first date.

The morning was still cool enough to be comfortable without his a/c on, and Christie soaked in the bustling sounds of the market crowds for a moment before sliding reluctantly out of his car. He pocketed his keys and glanced around for Robert's tall frame.

Well, shit.

Why hadn't they arranged a meeting place more specific than just at the market? Christie growled. He looked at his watch. It was *still* before 0800 on a Saturday, dammit.

A whiff of rich, darkly enticing heaven caught at his senses.

Christie mentally consigned Robert to the status of an evil minion of hell.

How had he talked Christie into getting up so damned early on a day it wasn't required of him?

Oh.

Right.

The evil fucker had slipped the question in right after the single best blow-job of Christie's life. While he could admire the pure Machiavellian brilliance of it, Christie refused to even attempt to look for Robert until he got some of that delicious smelling brew.

Turning slowly in a circle, Christie looked for a specific type of stand. It would have a long line. The people waiting would look sickly grey or angry and pale…basically like the undead. The people leaving the area would look relaxed, energized, and sort of post sex glowy.

There, at nine o'clock. That stand with the white awning over it was the place. Christie made a bee-line for the rosy-cheeked, smiling people. He drew closer. A dark-haired man laughed and talked a mile a minute as he served up liquid bliss. A zinging feeling shot along Christie's nerves. He drew in a deep breath and stepped into the line.

A man in a navy blue ball cap stepped into sight at the front of the line.

Hello.

Was that Robert?

It was difficult to tell what color his hair was. He was certainly tall enough to be Robert. Christie's eyes slipped down to rest on the man's ass.

Yes, that was definitely Robert. Christie made his way through the early morning coffee crowd toward the promise of a short-cut to freshly brewed coffee.

The delightful sight of Robert's oh so fine ass in a pair of well worn, tight fitting jeans was an added bonus. Robert's rich baritone voice was raspy as he thanked the man serving coffee. He turned from the table with not one, but two coffees in his big hands.

He smiled, his eyes lighting up when they landed on Christie.

"Your timing is impeccable. The coffee just finished brewing."

Robert stepped forward, bending down to brush a kiss over Christie's mouth. He held his hands out to the side, where there was no chance the hot liquid could spill on Christie. He stepped back just as quickly, a faint blush tingeing his cheeks.

The weight of the crowd's collective stares pressed against Christie's shoulders. Robert looked up and simply smiled wide at the gawkers, even winking, causing some of them to look away. Christie scanned their reactions quickly.

One rather buttoned up couple looked affronted, stalking off huffily.

An audacious lady in a silky looking, bright orange blouse winked back, giving him a thumbs-up signal. Her spiky silver pixie-cut and bright red lipstick somehow complemented the garish color of her blouse. The net effect was a youthfulness of spirit undaunted by her obviously advanced years. She blew them both a kiss before wandering off toward the pastry table where free samples of cinnamon rolls were being given away. Robert turned all his attention back to Christie, and his smile was still sweetly bashful but had kicked up a notch in intensity. He tugged on his ball cap, running a finger over the Yankee's logo on the front.

"The stuff to doctor up your coffee is right over here."

A smile tipped the corners of Christie's mouth. He really liked how Robert didn't hesitate to show he was excited to spend time together. Christie stepped over to the table, noting the coffee man had supplied his favorite type of creamer. Score.

"Thanks. I just need some sugar and a splash of cream."

Christie suited actions to words, stirring the ingredients into his drink and then puckering his lips to blow across the surface before taking a sip. An indrawn breath had him looking up to find Robert's eyes locked on his lips.

Robert drew in a deeper breath and sort of shook himself. A sheepish expression covered his face. A rueful smile followed as he pulled the lid off his coffee.

Watching as Robert added raw sugar but no cream, Christie sipped his coffee. God, it was amazing to not have to worry about Frankie pulling the hot liquid over on herself. It was so...freeing.

Robert had actually hooked him up with his new sitter. His niece Ally seemed like a good kid, and her references were great. While Christie adored Frankie, it had been really hard to go from being able to do whatever he wanted to suddenly having another person's wellbeing completely dependent on him.

Robert finished stirring his drink. Carefully placing the lid back on his cup, he smiled again.

"Come on, Christie. Let me show you the joys of shopping at the farmer's market."

Robert spun around and practically galloped toward a fruit stand a few feet from the coffee man. He picked up a cantaloupe, set his coffee down on the vendor's table and then flicked the melon while holding it to his ear.

Christie gaped at Robert for a second. His aunt Cate was always doing stuff like that, but he'd really never seen anyone else publicly abusing fruit. Christie laughed. Then he put the lid on his own coffee and followed the tall blond into the thick of the market.

Christie ran his hands over the incredibly soft surface of a purple, green, and lapis colored sweater. He shivered. This would feel incredible on, like being gently caressed by a thousand tiny fingers. This date was turning out to be a lot more fun than he'd anticipated. Christie turned his head to watch Robert walking among the stands of vegetables and baked goods nearby.

It felt good to just be in the moment.

The old lady who had given him the thumbs up stopped to check out the produce at a stand about half-way between him and Robert. She was evidently another fruit and vegetable abuser, poking at the tomatoes with a gnarled finger.

Christie smiled at her antics.

A slender boy wearing a ratty looking grey hoodie sidled up next to her. She pulled her big brightly patterned bag off her shoulder, setting it on the table next to her.

A frisson of uneasiness slid down Christie's back.

He tensed.

The kid snatched her bag up, spun around, and took off running.

He ran straight toward Christie.

Adrenaline surged into Christie's system like lightning. He stepped smoothly forward, snagging the kid's closer arm and hip-checking him.

Turning a wild, pale face toward Christie, he screamed in wordless rage.

Christie let the kid's momentum carry him up and over. He kept a firm grip on his arm, pulling up enough to keep the would-be robber's head from colliding with the pavement. As soon as the kid was all the way down, Christie dropped, winding his arms and legs around the now thrashing kid. Christie rolled onto his back, pulling the kid with him into the most easily maintainable hold he knew.

"Robert!"

Christie met the eyes of the kid—no, young man he was

restraining. The guy's eyes were huge and red rimmed, and he had a couple of day's growth of reddish brown beard on his face. He had to be at least four or five inches taller than Christie.

If he weighed more than a buck twenty-five Christie would eat that damned ball cap of Robert's though.

Shit.

"Why?"

The guy jolted like Christie had hit him with a tazer. His eyes welled up and he started to shake.

"I-I had to."

Christie looked into the amber depths of the young man's eyes. They were clear, the pupils a normal size. The sounds of the market crashed around them, a cacophony of raised voices. The guy whispered through dry, cracked lips.

"Please."

Sorrow cut at Christie, jagged edges eating into his gut. The muscles of his arms and legs loosened. The tired eyes above him widened, and the man tried to scramble off him.

"Not so damned fast, you."

Robert's big hand clamped down on the guy's shoulder.

"Christie, are you okay?"

A red hot jolt streaked through Christie's stomach.

"I'm fine Robert. Take it easy with him."

But Robert had already ripped the deceptively strong looking man off Christie, slamming him to the pavement, a knee in the center of his frail back.

Christie growled. Robert's trooper uniform might be a sexy shade of grey when he had it on, but it was clear the man couldn't see any other shade of grey.

"Jesus, Robert, go easy. He couldn't get out of the hold the lady put on him, you don't have to grind him into dust to keep him there."

Christie rolled to his feet, glaring at Robert as he scooped up the lady's bag. She was looking past him at the young man Robert held on the ground. She shook her head sadly.

"He used to model for my art classes. Oh, Aric, what happened to you?"

Christie froze.

"You know him?"

The old lady looked up at him, a bitterly reproachful expression on her face.

"Is it really necessary for the big man to hold him so... forcefully?"

Something equally bitter bloomed in Christie's chest.

"I would have said not, but he's the trooper, not me."

Her face paled.

"I won't press charges."

Sirens sounded in the distance.

"It might not matter. I really don't know what the laws are about this."

She moved around him, taking her bag with an elegant little nod of her head. She knelt down next to Robert.

"Aric, you could have come to me..."

She pressed a hand lightly to his shoulder.

"I just wanted your sketch pencils. I'm sorry, Mrs. Trask."

She reached into her bag, pulling out a handful of graphite artists pencils.

Robert put his hand out.

"Ma'am, you can't give those to him. He could use them as a weapon."

Later, Robert reached out to slide his hand into Christie's as they headed back to their cars. Christie stepped away, his gut still burning with anger. He stopped, folding his arms across his chest.

"Christ on a cracker, Robert; did you even think to question why anyone would attempt something so desperate? Life comes in lots of colors you know. It's not a damned black and white film, and that Yankees cap you're sporting is navy blue, not white, in case you hadn't noticed."

Robert flushed. He compressed his lips into a thin line, drawing in a deep breath.

"Christie, I'm an officer of the law. It's my duty to uphold the law."

Christie threw his hands up.

"Still with the black and white!"

He pinched the bridge of his nose.

"Robert, we'll just have to agree to disagree about whether what happened here today was a travesty of justice or not. I have to get home to my daughter."

Robert crowded in closer to him, his cerulean eyes questioning.

"Christie, I'm sorry our date got all fucked up. Let me make it up to you. I'll take you to the Symphony tonight."

Christie laughed.

"I don't think so. I like to give my sitter more notice than that."

Robert opened his mouth, and then closed it with a resigned sounding sigh. He nodded, watching Christie with sad eyes. He picked Christie's hand up, pressing the back against his chest.

"Drive safely, Christie."

Christie slid back into his car as reluctantly as he'd left it a few hours earlier. He put his key in the ignition, turned his car on, put it in gear, and drove away. Robert watched him the whole time, that sad expression never leaving his face.

Driving home, Christie turned the music up loud, and counted cows. He didn't want to think about the man he'd left behind, or their disagreement.

Twenty minutes after he dropped the sitter back at her house his phone rang.

"Hello."

"Christie. I. Uh, go check your mailbox."

Robert's warm baritone hesitated.

"Give him a chance, Christie."

Get out of my head Caro. I don't have time for this right now.

"Don't be so damn stubborn. You might miss out on more than you know."

"What?"

Christie pulled his phone away from his ear and stared at it accusingly.

"Sweet Goddess Christie; go check your mailbox and then call me back. If you want to, that is."

The connection cut off abruptly.

Bemused, Christie walked to his front door. A padded manila envelope stuck out of his mailbox. He tugged it out of the box. The package was squishy. Christie ripped it open.

Inside he found two tickets to the Symphony. The seats were some of the best in the house. The tickets rested on the purple, green, and blue sweater he'd admired at the farmer's market.

He pulled his phone back out of the pocket he'd shoved it into when Robert hung up on him. Christie pushed the little phone button, brought up his list of incoming calls, and hit the auto-dial function on his phone. Then he waited.

When the connection opened he didn't wait for Robert to speak.

"That's cheating, dammit."

"You'll go?"

Christie rolled his eyes. Machiavellian fucker.

"Yes."

CHAPTER SIX

Robert's second date with Christie had ended up a disaster. It was a miracle he'd managed to get the pissed off soldier to relent and grant him a third date. Taking Christie to the symphony and then dancing had been inspired. Now he needed to make sure their trip to the laser-tag arena got him even closer to his ultimate goal of winning Christie's affections.

Getting ready for his date with Christie should only take fifteen minutes, tops.

It took a good deal longer than that.

Fresh from the shower, Robert reached into his closet for a clean pair of jeans and accidently pulled out the suit he'd worn on their trip to the symphony.

The suit hadn't been to the cleaners yet.

It still smelled faintly like cucumber melon body-wash and espresso mixed with a hint of sweat and sex. It smelled like Christie.

Just that quickly, Robert was rock hard. He knew it was useless trying to slide into his favorite jeans until he took care of his rampant erection. He reached into his nightstand, pulled out an economy sized bottle of Astroglide, and set it in easy reaching distance. Then he lay back on his bed still holding the suit. He didn't care if it got a little dirtier before he sent it to be dry-cleaned. He didn't want to jump Christie at the range. His soldier was really looking forward to showing Robert some of those finely tuned Army skills of his, and Robert was determined to play nice.

Robert held the front of the jacket, where it had rubbed against Christie the most, up to his nose with one hand. With the other he pulled the towel around his waist loose and then squeezed a healthy dollop of lube directly onto his hot, stiff cock. The cool sensation sent a shiver through him, but the lube warmed quickly as he began to stroke himself while he let his mind drift back to the sizzling encounter he'd had with Christie in the restroom of the symphony. Robert closed his eyes and let the memory unfold against his inner eye.

Robert walked into the single occupancy handicapped bathroom in Christie's wake with numerous eyes burning into his back. The high, taut curve of his man's ass had drawn more eyes than just his. He'd slung the door open expecting Christie to be leaning back against the far wall, watching him with those hot 'fuck me now' eyes he got when he needed it badly.

"Sweet Goddess, fuck me."

"I was rather hoping you would fuck me, lover."

Christie's sultry, husky voice nearly made him whimper.

Christie was leaning against the wall alright, but not leaning back against it. Instead the hot little fucker had his shoulders and chest against the wall, his face turned to one side, beautiful suit pants around his ankles, and both hands clasping his firm round buttocks, spreading himself for his lover. The black base of a butt plug was stretching his hole, a shimmer of lube catching the lobby lights and reflecting them back. A lustful groan from immediately behind him to the left and a shocked gasp from somewhere slightly farther behind and to the right broke the spell just enough for him to step forward into the darkened room and shut the door.

Robert locked the door with one hand while the other flipped the light switch to the on position. Then he was across the room, ripping his pants open, easing the plug out, and plunging into Christie's hot depths again and again and again. He didn't stop until Christie was screaming into the impromptu gag he'd made out of his forearm and the black camelhair blazer covering it, until he had pumped every drop of semen in his balls out into Christie's hot, clasping depths. Then he pulled Christie back from the wall by his hips until the man had enough room to reach down and grasp his ankles. He eased his cock out and filled Christie back up with the plug.

Robert admired his handiwork for a moment. He was damned glad they'd gotten their test results back today. Bending down, he grabbed a handful of the longer hair on top of Christie's head and pulled him up by it. He didn't release it when Christie was fully upright, instead continuing to pull until Christie stood arched back against him. He let Christie feel the precariousness of his position for a single heartbeat.

"You'll leave the plug there until I take it out." Robert pressed hard against Christie's naked backside. "I think I'll take you dancing when the symphony is over. I want to watch you writhing on a dance floor with my come bottled up inside you, baby."

As the memory came to a conclusion, Robert's balls drew tight and shot their load all over his chest, abdomen, and the now incredibly filthy suit jacket. He shook with the release, his breaths coming in short, ragged bursts. Robert opened his eyes back up and grinned to himself. He used the jacket to mop himself up, knowing he didn't have time for another shower if he was going to be on time to get Christie.

Yeah, their trip to the symphony had been a stellar date.

Robert started thinking up ways to make this trip to Lasertron just as much fun...without getting either of them arrested. An evil, wickedly wonderful thought flowed into his mind. Robert smiled as he pulled his toy box from under the bed. He opened it, rifling through until he found what he was looking for.

Heh.

Vibrating cock rings with remote controls.

Yeah, that should take Lasertron to the next level.

It might even screw with Christie's aim enough to give him a prayer of winning.

He whistled John Mayer's *Your Body is a Wonderland* all the way to Christie's house.

Robert grinned at himself in the mirror. Three months. Christie had held out three whole months before he would agree to meet Robert's parents. Robert had finally worn him down though, and tonight was the night he would finally be able to present his *sjelefrende*, his soul mate to his parents. His eyes scanned the outfit he was wearing. It was the fourth he'd tried on tonight. He usually had no trouble deciding what to wear, but couldn't seem to settle on whether he wanted casual elegance or formality tonight. He shook his head, stripped off the blue silk club shirt he was wearing, and picked up his phone. He punched number one on his speed dial and waited impatiently for the sweetly husky voice of his lover to answer.

"Hello?"

"Christie, what are you wearing?"

"Christ on a cracker Robert, this is no time for phone sex. We're due at your parents in an hour and twenty-five minutes, and it'll take a good hour for us to get up there."

Robert laughed. Trust Christie to think he had his mind in the gutter. Goddess knew most of the time the man would be correct. Pretty much whenever he was in Christie's presence he wanted to have sex with him. Even if it was just over the phone, sex with Christie was a not to be missed event.

"No babe, no...I swear I'm not trying to get in your pants right now. Tonight I'm just trying to figure out what to wear."

There was a weighted silence from the other end of the line. Robert heard an odd scraping noise intermittently in the background.

"I can't figure out what to wear either! Shit. I never had to meet someone's parents before!"

Christie sounded frazzled. The scraping noise came again, and this time Robert realized it was the sound of hangers being pushed along the metal rod of the closet in Christie's bedroom. Robert thought quickly. He came up with a solution he thought would work to take the strain off them both.

"Christie, what's your favorite outfit of mine?"

"Huh? Oh... I pick your outfit and you pick mine... genius.

I like that blue silk shirt with the black jeans that show off your butt. Wear them with the black camelhair blazer. If you wear that outfit, I'll be too busy drooling over you to be nervous about meeting your parents."

Robert closed his eyes and pictured Christie.

Oh. "Wear the outfit you had on when I took you to the symphony Christie. I love that outfit."

The black turtleneck with the black jacket and black slacks made his voice rasp.

Robert heard Christie giggle, and then start to hum a very familiar little tune. He knew exactly what Christie was thinking of. Robert shook his head to clear it of the lust filled haze. He cupped his cock, giving one slow stroke of promise. He knew he had to nip this in the bud, or his wanton baby would end up spread across his mother's dining room table, and while Robert was fairly sure his mother would forgive him for embarrassing her eventually, he knew his father would not.

"Get those wonderfully slutty notions out of your head Christie. At least until dinner's over and we can get back to your place. I'd hate to drag you out of my parent's house half-way through dinner only to get arrested for having sex on the side of the highway by one of my fellow troopers."

Christie giggled again. This time Robert recognized his 'I'll behave on the outside and think slutty thoughts on the inside' giggle. It was his second favorite sound that Christie made.

Christie's first hint that Robert was just about as nervous as he was about the whole meeting the parents deal came when they pulled up in front of the sprawling farmhouse the elder Lindstroms resided in. There were only a few extra cars strewn along the sides of the driveway and lined up in the open space next to the barn. He turned in his seat to find Robert counting the cars. A slight tic started to pulsate under his right eye. Christie watched as the tic grew more pronounced. Robert compressed his lips into what Christie had come to think of as his grimly resigned look. Robert shrugged, turned his head, and as he met Christie's eyes the look melted into one of apology.

"I didn't know Bergitta and Nikki would both be here. I'm sorry; I would have warned you if I'd known. Things tend to get a little tense when they're both around at the same time. I don't know what mom was thinking."

Robert heaved a put upon sigh. Christie bit his lip and cleared his throat. He reached over and patted Robert's leg.

"It'll be fine Robert. As long as they aren't baby eating cannibals, we'll be fine."

He turned to peek back through the crack in between the front seats.

"Won't we Frankie?"

The baby threw her stuffed bear on the floor of the car.

"Bey-ar!"

Christie looked back at Robert as he snagged the ragged bear off the floorboards and handed it back to Frankie. The big man was muttering to himself. It actually sounded like he said he wasn't sure about Bergitta. Christie squeezed his thigh, arching a brow at his lover.

"We have to go in Robert; they already know we're here. That's your brother Sven peeking out the curtains. He's likely already told them that he sees your car, and if they don't see us coming in pretty soon, they'll think something's wrong."

Robert grunted and actually pouted.

"I hate it when they fight, Christie."

Christie lifted his hand from Robert's thigh, gripping his chin and turning his head to look into his eyes.

"Then we won't let them fight."

A movement on the porch caught Christie's attention. Christ on a cracker, it looked like the scaled down version of the cast of Beverly Hills 90210-the Scandinavian edition had just popped up on Robert's parent's porch. They all looked…well bred, well bleached, and potentially lethal. The two youngest women were standing at opposite ends of the family grouping, tension still crackling between them. A chuckle managed to escape him. It looked like dealing with Robert's family would be more exciting than a day at the AT4 range blowing stuff up.

A warm hand closed over his. Christie paused in his perusal of the Lindstroms on the porch for a moment. Robert was smiling at him, but the little crinkle in-between his brows said he was puzzled. The crinkle smoothed out, and Robert tilted his head to one side.

"Christie, don't they faze you even a little?"

Christie swallowed. He tried to pick the least freakish thing to say. He didn't think they'd been dating long enough to share all their little psychoses yet.

"Robert, even if your sisters get into a brawl it's only going to make me uncomfortable for your sake. I get that you love them both, and it hurts you when they fight. Personally...I love watching stuff explode. When those two tangle?"

He pointed to first Nikki and then to Bergitta.

"It's gonna be better than a day at the AT4 range. Even though both your sisters look dangerous, my money's on Nikki. It's always the little ones who turn out to be more dangerous. Don't worry though, I'll step in if it looks like they're actually gonna do permanent damage."

Robert didn't say anything for a moment. His hot blue gaze pierced Christie with its intensity. It made Christie twitch, and he started to open his mouth to say something, anything to fill the silence quickly boiling up between them. Robert laid a finger over his mouth and pressed lightly down.

"I love you, Christie."

Christie took a moment to think about that. Then he nodded his head decisively.

"That's a good thing Mr. Lindstrom, because I love you too."

Christie opened the passenger side door then, and slide

sinuously out of his seat. He turned and leaned down to glance at Robert through the still open door, a mischievous grin on his face.

"Last one to the porch gets cuffed to the bed tonight."

Robert scrambled out of the car and strode quickly up to the top of the porch steps, giving his gran a hug before turning back to blow Christie a kiss. Christie didn't even realize he'd reached up to catch it until a delighted grin chased across Robert's face.

Chuckling because Robert had been diverted exactly as he'd hoped he would be, Christie shut his door and set about pulling Frankie and all her accoutrements out of the back seat. She stopped fussing as soon as he unbuckled her and pulled her up into his arms. Stepping back with everything in his arms, he bumped the car door shut with his hip. When Christie straightened up he found himself eye to eye with Robert's fierce looking eldest sister. The pinched cast to her mouth let him know that meeting her wasn't likely to be as pleasant as meeting Ally's mom had been.

"You must be Bergitta."

CHAPTER SEVEN

Bergitta Lindstrom was actually a very beautiful woman. She looked just like Robert. Christie saw an angry, lost look in her eyes that he'd never seen in his lover's though.

She sniffed at him. Not in a, gee, you smell terrific; what is that cologne you're wearing kind of sniff. No. This was an, oh, there's dog crap on my shoe sort of sniff. Christie bristled a bit.

She arched an eyebrow at him.

"Where's the baby's mother?"

Christie bit back the first response that came to mind. He'd seen Caro be every bit as surly with the few dates he'd brought home to the apartment he'd shared with her.

"She's dead."

She paled slightly at that. She pressed her lips together even harder than before, until they were nearly bloodless.

"I'm...sorry for your loss, Mr. Collins. You must miss her a great deal. Had you been married long?"

Christie smiled at her. It was as though they were the only ones present on the whole farm, just the two of them and Frankie, caught in a little bubble of time. Bergitta looked down as she spoke, a hectic flush rising in her cheeks. She looked so much like Robert when he was righteously angry that Christie couldn't bring himself to be ungracious with her.

"Bergitta, I miss Caro every day. It was a terrible loss, for both Frankie and I. Caro was my best friend in the world, and I loved her very much, but it would have been a mockery of the institution for us to marry. I don't think that's really the point you were trying to make though, was it?"

Christie scanned the porch over Bergitta's shoulder. Robert was ushering a protesting Nikki inside rather forcefully. Well, this was as good a time as any to find out what Bergitta's problem really was.

"So what is it Bergitta? Do you think I'm too young for Robert? Or maybe you think I'm just not good enough?"

Bergitta's eyes glittered with feeling.

"I think you're going to let him fall in love with you and your baby and then break his heart."

Frankie whined, tucking her head into his neck as though hiding. She dropped her bear again, letting out a distressed sounding wail. Christie shifted Frankie higher on his shoulder. Damn. He'd forgotten that while she might not understand the words, she'd shown him repeatedly that she picked up on emotions and levels of tension very well.

"I'm not going to have this conversation in front of my daughter Bergitta. Right now I could use some help with Frankie. I didn't know if your mom would have a playpen, so I brought our travel one. I can't carry the baby, the playpen, and the diaper bag safely though…and Robert appears to have abandoned me. Could you carry Frankie for me?"

Bergitta's mouth fell open, and her eyes locked on Christie's. He squatted down, grabbed Bey-ar, and stood back up. Beating the bear against his thigh to knock all the dust off, he handed it back to Frankie.

"You would trust me with your baby? But we just met, and I…"

Christie gave her his most charming grin.

"Well, I'm pretty sure Robert knows where you live, and I swear that man is more protective of Frankie than I am. I'm pretty sure it'll be fine. Besides, you don't strike me as the type that would take her ire out on an innocent baby."

Bergitta stared at him for a moment. She reached out hesitantly, and Christie passed Frankie over. The baby looked up from gnawing on Bey-ar's foot, spied a long strand of shining blond hair, and promptly grabbed for it with both hands, dropping Bey-ar in the process.

Christie caught the stuffed bear.

"No, no baby. It's not nice to pull hair. Come on, I'll give you…"

Bergitta swung around from where she'd already started walking toward the house.

"Does she eat cookies yet?"

Christie shrugged.

"I've only given her the ones they make for babies…I guess as long as it's not too sweet or too hard to chew she should be fine."

Bergitta gave a reserved smile and turned back toward the house. Christie watched her go for a moment, and then walked to the trunk of Robert's car, opening it with the spare key Robert had given him last month. He pulled the portable playpen out and followed Robert's eldest sister into the house, wondering why his lover had acted as if she were such a fearsome figure, and muttering to himself..

"Jeez. You'd have thought the woman would turn out to be an avenging Valkyrie or something the way Robert went on about her. She's really not that bad once you get past that surface prickliness, just kind of bitchily protective. I'll bet there's quite a story there."

Christie strode up the path to the wide front porch chuckling as he imagined Bergitta as a big hedgehog in a matronly apron.

Twenty five minutes later Christie managed to politely escape Robert's mother. Petra Lindstrom's gentle interrogation had actually put him at ease, but he'd had enough of it for one session. Extracting himself with a sudden urgent need to check on Frankie, he managed to hunt Robert down. He dragged his lover out to the car for a moment of privacy in which to bend Robert's ear concerning the size of his immediate family, stashing a napping Frankie in her car seat.

"Christ on a cracker, Robert! How many siblings do you

have?"

Robert grinned. The man was such a smart ass. Maybe he could develop the trait as a self preservation technique for survival in Robert's big family.

"Thirteen. I have five sisters and eight brothers. Mom was trying for seven girls, but she gave up after the ninth boy. She said she had better than a baker's dozen all together, and that was enough for anyone."

Christie gaped at him again. He noted how Robert watched his mouth open and close. Christie knew the motion was almost identical to what he did with his mouth when he was in the throes of an orgasm. Robert shifted in his seat, looking increasingly uncomfortable. Christie glanced down to take in Robert's sexy black jeans. They were growing noticeably tighter. He looked back up, arching an eyebrow at Robert.

Robert shrugged. "I can't help it, Christie. You made the same face you make when you're—umm really enjoying yourself with me."

When Christie finally followed Robert's gaze to the mirror, Robert mouthed the words 'little pitchers' and nudged his chin as comically as possible in the direction of the back seat. He had to know it would look silly. Christie thought he probably wanted it to look silly. It certainly got Christie to crack up.

Robert glanced up at the house. Following the direction of his gaze, Christie saw the living room window's curtains twitch, and knew someone in the Lindstrom clan was watching them. He gulped. He and Robert probably had mere moments to get out of the car on their own before someone was sent to round them up and usher them into the presence of Robert's mother, father, gran, and assorted siblings.

"Uh, Christie, they're gonna descend on us if we don't get out of the car and bring the baby back inside. It really was a tactical error on your part to bring her out with us. They'd have probably given us a half an hour or so to ourselves if we'd left Frankie where they could spoil her."

Christie nodded his head sagely. Then he shot Robert a wicked grin.

"I know. I brought her out to chaperone us."

Robert gave him a surprised look. Then he unbuckled and cracked his door open before pausing.

"And Christie?"

"Yeah Robert?"

"Don't let yourself get cornered by my mom or my sister Bergitta. They'll have every bit of information about yourself you ever thought private sucked out and being delicately dissected between the two of them in under a minute flat."

Christie rolled his eyes.

"They're not that bad Robert."

Robert arched an eyebrow.

"Wanna bet a week's worth of handcuff time?"

Christie got hot just thinking of having Robert at his mercy for a whole week.

"You're on, Robert."

Robert smirked at him.

"How does my mother know we had sex in the bathroom at the symphony?"

With that said, Robert hopped out of the car, hustled around to the other side of the car and hauled Frankie out of the back seat.

He stopped on the porch and waited. After a moment, Christie crawled out of his side of the car. Robert smiled at his man. Christie scowled back at him. Robert laughed.

Christie pursed his lips. He squinted aggrievedly up at Robert. Then an unholy joy seemed to light him from within.

"You set me up Robert...I think that means you have to wear the handcuffs tonight anyway."

His mouth was still open when Christie spotted a slightly

shocked looking Bergitta standing off to one side on the porch. He snapped his jaw shut. Robert half turned and addressed his sister wryly over his shoulder.

"Merry meet again, Bergitta. Are you dressed up as death again? Cause I swear the last time I saw someone look at you with such abject terror was the day you nearly gave that poor trick-or-treater a lasting fear of the entire holiday."

A solid smack landed on the back of Robert's head. Bergitta cleared her throat. Robert turned fully toward her and stage whispered.

"Not a word about what Christie just said, or I'll tell mom what you and Bobby Rinehart were really doing in the barn all those times she thought he was helping you curry the horses."

Bergitta looked at him with a shocked expression. She pressed her lips into a thin line, crossed her eyes, stuck her tongue out at him, and then stepped smoothly around him. Robert continued into the house chortling. Christie shook his head.

"I can dress him up, but the manners are still a work in progress, Bergitta. If you'll excuse me, I need to make sure he settles Frankie somewhere safe."

Christie hurried in after Robert. He'd really rather have it out with Bergitta after dinner, so if things got ugly he wouldn't miss out on Mrs. Lindstrom's cooking. Robert had been raving about it for weeks, and Christie really wanted a chance to try out some of her Swedish delicacies.

CHAPTER EIGHT

Christie spotted his weaselly lover across the room. Hah. Grab the baby and run while sacrificing Christie to the tender mercies of the high inquisitor of the Lindstrom family would he? Later, much later, Robert was going to pay in spades for that.

Christie flipped open his phone and checked the date. It was the 5th of the month. If that 'throw Christie under the bus' fucker wanted back in his ass before next month, he'd better plan on spending the next week or so handcuffed to the bed and tortured whenever he wasn't at work. He shouldn't have left Christie to explain or duck explaining what Bergitta had overheard. It wasn't like Christie was the one with oodles of sister handling experience.

"High inquisitor? Really Christie? With all that blond hair and the tawny-gold skin I'd have gone for the lioness visual."

Shut up for just a moment, Caro. Unless, of course, you have ideas about how I can best torture Robert.

"Look Christie, Robert's Gran is holding Frankie... that's sweet isn't it?"

Christie sighed. Trust Caro to go right for the heart of the matter. He addressed her again in his head.

Okay Caro, point made. I'll call a cease-fire for now. We wouldn't want any non-combatants to get caught in the cross-fire. I'll go meet his Gran. We can declare her and the baby Switzerland. Robert calls his gran Switzerland anyway...says she's neutral territory and minor squabbles aren't allowed to infringe on her territory.

"Cute Christie, real cute...what's Robert then?"

That boyfriend abandoning fucker is Kosovo. Full of starving peasants and unexploded landmines he is.

Caro snorted loud enough for the person standing in front of Christie to turn and look questioningly at him. He gave a slightly chagrined smile, gave the Lindstrom greeting of 'merry meet', and continued making his way across the room toward Robert's Gran Olava. Several children were darting through the room, weaving an indecipherable path around the grown-ups. Christie wasn't sure exactly how many there were. He narrowed his eyes and tried to count them for the umpteenth time. There couldn't be more than four or five mini-Lindstroms tearing through the house. They all looked too much alike and were moving too quickly for him to be sure he had an accurate count however. He eased around them and slid up next to Robert, giving the bigger man a surreptitious pinch on his side for leaving Christie in an embarrassing situation.

"Robert, is this the beloved grandmother whom you've told me so much about?"

Robert snorted. Christie's out-of-breath, trying not to show he was irritated sounding voice must have sounded hilarious to the man. Robert gave his Gran a wink with the eye closest to Christie.

"Gran, I explained to Christie how you're sort of like Switzerland here. We're all safe in the neutral zone of your influence."

Robert edged slightly away from Christie as he spoke. Christie let him go. He'd have plenty of time later to pay Robert back for his sly little trick.

Christie was amazed to see the elderly woman give Robert an exaggerated wink back before she replied, in a too loud voice.

"Why that's true enough *barnebarn*! Tell me Robbie, when are you going to marry this young man so I can tell everyone I have yet another beautiful little great granddaughter?"

Robert grinned openly at her now. Christie smirked and shook his head at the way they were hamming it up. It was obvious they had rehearsed this exchange. Robert's mother squealed in delight and a chorus of voices broke out demanding to know when and where the wedding was going to take place. Robert's father quickly offered to let them have it under the "Great Oak". Christie narrowed his eyes at Robert. The boyfriend abandoner had the audacity to wink at him.

"Gran, I'm working on it, but these things take time."

"Hah…I knew it…He wants to kiss you, he wants to hold you, and he wants to marry you…"

Give it a rest Caro. Isn't it a national ghost matchmaker's holiday or something?

Caro just sniffed again.

After dinner Bergitta managed to cull Christie from the herd in the living room and cunningly maneuvered him toward the French doors onto the side porch. Robert started toward them, but Christie waved him away. He had a feeling that he'd get more of the real reasons behind her antagonism without Robert present.

Just as he reached the door, he caught Gran Olava's eye.

"Keep Robert away." He barely mouthed the phrase, but he was gratified to see her approving nod. Then he allowed Bergitta to usher him out the doors and onto the side porch. Once they were outside and the doors were secured behind them, Christie swung around.

"Well, Bergitta, what did you want to speak with me about?"

Christie watched as Bergitta's mouth tightened mutinously. He sighed. According to Robert, she really did mean well…but she was so intense, and so firmly of the belief that there wasn't a man or woman out there worthy of her brothers and sisters. In his case she even figured she had proof of that, because how could a gay man have a daughter? Roll those things together and it made her pure evil to deal with.

"I expect this is the moment when you tell me again why I'm not good enough for Robert and follow it up with a statement about how if I care for him at all I'll leave him alone. How many of Robert's boyfriends have you run off with this speech, Bergitta?"

"You don't know what you're talking about." Bergitta's face

flushed, her knuckles clenched white and shaking. "I don't run anyone away. I know things my brothers and sisters don't. I protect them!"

Christie arched a brow at her. Dealing with her was like driving a load of unstable nitroglycerin down a dirt road in the spring. Suicide. Robert's wonder at Christie's lack of fear in dealing with her began to make a great deal more sense.

"What don't they know, Bergitta?"

"They don't know you have to test people first; that most people lie and cheat. My family is good." Darkness ghosted across Bergitta's eyes. "They don't see the badness in others."

Bergitta wasn't talking about him anymore.

"And you do, Bergitta?" Christie softened his voice, but she still spun as if struck, placing her back to him while wrapping her hands around her middle.

"Why did you let me take your baby?"

"I answered that earlier, Bergitta. What do you know that your brothers and sisters don't?"

Bergitta's shoulders hunched.

"Nikki knows."

Both of Christie's brows rose at that. Christ on a cracker, what was it about him that had everyone spilling their guts to him?

"My boyfriend…I didn't know he was watching Nikki." Bergitta focused her confession on the potted fern in front of her, her voice almost too soft to hear. "She… She was fifteen. So pretty. Like now. He… She snuck out to a party. Drank too much. And he was there. She trusted him because he was my boyfriend. He gave her more alcohol…and when she passed out he…he… He's Ally's father."

Christie sucked in a hard breath as hot shards of pain flowered open in his chest. No wonder she didn't trust anyone outside her family.

"Bergitta, turn around."

She turned slowly, biting her lip so hard it was a wonder she hadn't bitten right through it.

"Anything you want to ask about me, or my intentions toward Robert, you feel free to go right ahead and ask. I get you might need that."

Bergitta nodded tightly. Then she turned again, and strode off the porch, heading for the barn. Christie watched her go, his heart aching for her.

"Gran, you're supposed to be on my side."

Gran Olava smiled serenely at Robert.

"Ah, Robbie; I am on your side. Your boy has to stand up to Bergitta on his own, or she will never accept him. Stop fussing and go find Nikolina. She could likely do with a friendly adult face...I think she got stuck watching the little ones again."

His gran calmly patted his hand before releasing it with a shooing motion. Robert gave in, kissed her wrinkled cheek, and headed off to find Nikki. When he found the area where the rugrats had been put on lock down he found his brother Sven had relived her fifteen minutes ago.

"Sorry Robert. She took off like a shot. I heard her mustang starting up...I'm pretty sure she's gone home already."

Robert couldn't get mad. Sven had his own two toddlers climbing him like a jungle-gym while he burped Frankie against one shoulder. What he was right now was confused. Ally-Cat was still in the front room with his mom and dad. Nikki would never take off without her daughter.

"Thanks, Sven. I'll just call her."

Walking out to the back porch, Robert whipped out his cell-phone and hit speed-dial number two. Nikki picked up on the second ring.

"Nikolina, I hope you have your headset on. I'd hate to have to write you a ticket for driving and talking on the cell-phone without one."

A snort came over the line.

"What do you want Robert?"

Robert wasn't above groveling to get what he wanted.

"You. I want you to come back. Why did you abandon me?"

Nikki laughed.

"Poor baby, did your man run screaming for the hills after having to socialize with so many Lindstroms at once? Tell me you didn't actually tell him how many of us there are. You do know Sven kept his Margie in the dark about that until after the actual vows were said right?"

"It's not right that you take such joy in my trials, Nikki. Bergitta took him off to interrogate, and Gran wouldn't let me intervene."

She snorted some more.

"Listen Robert, seriously, I think Christie can hold his own. Besides, I just ran to get some praline ice cream for mom. Dad ate the last of it and he forgot to replace it."

Robert whistled.

"Ooomph. That's a hangin' offense in these parts."

Robert practically heard her grinning over the phone.

"I know. That's why I snuck out. We're hoping to get it into the freezer before mom notices."

Robert laughed.

"Pick up some vanilla for me?"

"Robert, you know mom keeps vanilla in the freezer for you."

Robert nodded his head, and then remembered Nikki couldn't see him.

"I know Nikki. This is for when I tie Christie up tonight."

There was a long pause.

"Does Christie know you spread his business around like this?"

Robert rolled his eyes.

"Nikki, I'd never say that to anyone but you."

Another silence weighed down the line.

"Ah, but Robert, how will you buy my silence?"

Robert's mouth dropped open.

He sputtered.

"You…you wouldn't dare!"

Nikki laughed.

"Nah, I'd never do that to Christie. Alyssa loves him too much. But I will tell Christie about—"

"Nikki, what do you want?"

"I need a sitter for Saturday night. I've got a date."

Robert blew out a mildly irritated breath.

"Fine. We were going to stay in that night anyway. You didn't have to blackmail me, you know. I love spending time with Ally."

Nikki giggled.

"I know. I just enjoy blackmailing you. I'll be back in a bit with the ice cream. Try to keep mom away from the freezer 'til I get back, 'kay?"

"Okay, Nikki. Bye."

"Bye."

CHAPTER NINE

As soon as the first sergeant said the words, "Orders have come down from…" Christie knew his unit was getting deployed sometime soon. He had updated his will when Frankie came to live with him, but he still needed to get to Legal. There would need to be changes made to who his beneficiaries were, as well as a power of attorney to draw up for whoever was going to be keeping his little mouse while he was gone. He needed to talk to Robert about all this stuff.

Specialist Evans fell into step next to him as soon as they were released for the end of day formation. Evans had transferred in from a unit in Germany a little while before Christie got Frankie, and he was still having a little trouble fitting into the unit. He'd caught a bit of flak from some of the less liberal guys since his two dads had come to visit him one weekend on post.

"Yeah, so Collins, can I still get a ride into town with you tonight? I need to pick my car up from the shop. Man, I am so glad our squad leader didn't put you on extra duty over that whole speeding ticket-going to court during duty-hours thing. None of these other punks in our squad would want to be seen with me in their car."

Christie was also thankful he'd managed to stay out of trouble on the court date thing. He nodded at his buddy, still worrying about how to break the news to Robert.

"No worries Evans. We just need to hurry because my boyfriend has the late shift tonight and I want to let him know what's going on before he goes to work. I don't want him to hear about this from someone else."

Evans tilted his head as he got into Christie's car, and smiled a little half smile at him.

"Thanks, man."

Christie laughed. Sometimes Evans slipped into treating him

the way he'd observed the other man treating girls he was hitting on. Evans said it was because Christie was so damn cute. Usually it annoyed Christie, but today it was a welcome relief from his concern over how Robert was going to take the news, and how a long separation was going to affect them as a couple.

"Stop flirting with me Evans, before I have to tell my big bad state trooper about it. You know he'd get all his cop buddies to harass you."

Evans held his hands up in mock surrender. He kept up a light banter all the way into town. Only when Christie dropped the other soldier off at the body shop in town where he needed to pick his car up did Evans turn a serious look on Christie.

"See ya then Collins. I hope your guy doesn't get too freaked out about the deployment. That's what my last girlfriend broke up with me over. She said she couldn't take living in limbo while she waited to see if I was even going to make it home. I… Well, I really hope your guy takes it better, man."

Christie nodded at Evans. He wasn't about to try talking when he knew he might come out sounding like a pubescent boy going through a voice change. Evans nodded back, and thumped the top of the car after he shut the passenger side door.

Swallowing hard, Christie put his car in gear and drove away. He hoped Robert took it better than that too. Every day he fell a little more in love with the guy. He didn't know what he'd do if Robert couldn't hack him getting deployed.

Robert looked at the table setting with satisfaction. They were coming up on their six month anniversary…well, if you counted from the first time he'd laid eyes on Christie. He figured since he'd known from that exact moment they were destined to be together, it should count as their anniversary date.

Fuck it; even if Christie didn't agree about the date, it was going to be a great night anyway. Tonight was the night. Robert was pretty sure Christie had totally forgiven him for leaving when Bergitta overheard their handcuff discussion. Oh, yeah, tonight was the night Robert was going to ask Christie to marry him.

As soon as he heard the garage door go up he lit the candles, stripped down to his skin, and tied the engagement ring he'd bought Christie to his cock with the gold and black striped silk ribbon he'd bought especially for tonight. He figured Christie would appreciate the nod to the Army colors, and he thought they were auspicious colors in general. Plus he knew Christie would get a kick out of his engagement ring being a "cock ring". He had another gift for Christie in the bedroom, but his sexy man was going to have to earn that one.

Christie walked in through the door that connected to the garage.

"Hey babe. You alone tonight?" It didn't hurt to check and make sure he hadn't brought any of his Army buddies home with him.

Christie made a muffled sound. Ah, he must be getting undressed out in the laundry room. Perfect.

"I made a salad, and figured we could grill some steaks once you unwrap the present I got for you."

Christie came through the laundry room door, a brow cocked in query as he started to unbutton his camouflage pants. His sleek chest and gorgeous, taut abs had Robert's ribbon quickly acting as a very real cock ring. Robert was seated at the table, so Christie hadn't seen he was nearly naked yet. The hungry way Christie was watching Robert's chest promised there was a good chance he'd be more than willing to fall in with Robert's plans for the evening.

Christie's face lit up.

"Present? You have a present for me? Where is it?"

Robert grinned. He loved the way Christie got so excited about little things. He brought the guy a cheap plastic toy from a fast food restaurant where he'd picked up his lunch one day, and Christie had been over the moon. It was cute. He'd never tell Christie that, because then they'd probably fight over whether or not Christie was cute—which he unequivocally was, and that would be a waste of time.

"I've got your present right here babe…and you've got all night to play with it…I switched shifts with Evan Carrollton, and sent Frankie over to Nikolina's with Ally."

Robert pushed his chair back. Christie looked down. Robert knew he was expecting a present to be hidden in Robert's lap. Watching Christie's eyes go smoky with desire, and his cheeks flush with color, had Robert's cock hardening even more. Christie licked his lips. He continued walking forward. Robert waited patiently until he got close enough and then—

"Gotcha, babe."

Robert led Christie's hand down to the end of the ribbon the ring was dangling from. Christie's eyes went from smoky to startled. Robert had deliberately tied the ring loosely, so when Christie tugged on it, it came loose in his hand.

Christie brought his hand slowly up to his waist level and clenched it shut in a fist. Robert took hold of his wrist, turning his palm up toward the ceiling. Then he uncurled Christie's fingers one by one.

"A ring, Robert?"

"An engagement ring, Christie. If you'll take it."

Christie swallowed hard. He didn't answer.

"Christie Collins, will you marry me?"

Christie still didn't say anything.

Robert's gut twisted up. He squeezed his eyes shut. Shit. He'd gotten it wrong somehow. He'd pushed Christie too fast. He—

"Yes, Robert. Oh, hell, yes."

Robert's eyes popped open. He grabbed Christie's hips, pulling him in close. Air flowed into his lungs again, and along with it the most delicious scent. Christie smelled hot, musky, and faintly of the cucumber melon body wash he used every morning.

"Shit Christie, you scared me. I thought you were going to say no."

"Yeah, well. I couldn't breathe for a minute."

Robert looked up into Christie's eyes. Their blue-green depths were glittering with a film of moisture. Robert closed his own eyes to savor the moment, burying his face in Christie's stomach and breathing deeply of his fiancés unique scent.

Goddess, what the scent of cucumbers and melons did to Robert was nearly cause for a charge of public indecency.

Christie moaned when Robert nuzzled into the open vee of the smaller man's half unbuttoned cargo pants. Robert opened his mouth to taste the faintly salty skin of Christie's belly. He nipped gently at the ridge of Christie's hip, causing a catch in the other man's voice as he spoke.

"Well, Trooper Lindstrom, what do you plan to do with me now that you have me?"

Robert groaned right back. Oh, he knew that tone. That was the sound of slutty Christie coming out to play. He grabbed the base of his cock to stop himself from coming too quickly.

"Why Trooper Lindstrom, I think you like it when I talk slutty."

"You know I do, Christie."

Robert pressed a moist kiss to the tender skin accessible above the low riding cargo pants. Then he bit down, unable to resist the heady feeling it gave him to leave marks on his man. Christie shouted and tried to jump back. Robert held on, gentling the bite into a sucking kiss, holding on until he managed to suck up a dark mark. Then he allowed Christie to move back slightly. He admired the visible proof of his connection to his soldier. Then Robert released Christie's hips, pulling the other man's hands from his shoulders and placing them on the partially undone fly.

"Finish taking them off babe. I want to taste you."

Christie sucked in a sharp breath and pulled on the sides of his fly. Buttons popped, some sliding free, some coming loose as threads tore and then dropping to the floor. His pants dropped around his ankles. Robert bent his head, licking a line up the side of Christie's cock. He made sure to get a solid grip on the smaller man's hips and then wrapped his lips around the leaking head of

Christie's shaft. Robert moaned as Christie's length slid through his lips and across his tongue. The sweet and salty taste of his lover's pre-come drove him wild, tearing another groan from his throat. Christie made a strangled sound as his knees gave way. Robert pulled off for a moment, grinning up at his dazed lover.

"It's like knowing the secret short cut on a video game babe. Every time I suck you all the way down, you lose control of your legs. Damn I love that."

Christie thrust his hips forward. He squinted evilly down at Robert.

"Robert, you need to do more sucking and less talking."

Robert grinned harder, winked up at Christie, and proceeded to suck him down to the root again. He hummed his favorite Nine Inch Nails song, *'Fuck You Like an Animal'*, while letting his tongue play with the silky skin covering Christie's iron hard shaft. Pulling off until only the head still rested in his mouth, Robert dipped his tongue into the slit, searching for more of the sweetly salty fluid he'd tasted earlier.

Christie started to babble above him, and Robert reveled in the incredible feeling of reducing his fierce warrior to incoherence. Flicking his tongue along the bottom of Christie's shaft, he traced the fat vein running up it. Goddess, he absolutely loved the feel of Christie coming unhinged in his mouth. Robert stopped to pay special, loving attention to the spot just under the head. He worried the cluster of nerves there with his lips and tongue, loving the faint bumpiness of the spot against the sensitive flesh of his mouth. Then Robert opened up his mouth, placed his teeth carefully right under the edge of the helmet, and bit down just slightly. That pushed Christie over the edge. He came screaming Robert's name.

CHAPTER TEN

Christie knew he must have screamed Robert's name out again. His throat was raw in the way it got when he'd been screaming. Not remembering how he got into the bedroom was a new one though. He vaguely remembered Robert picking him up. He didn't remember getting strapped into this interesting position though. His legs were spread up and out, and there were straps running under his back suspending him above the bed. He was a little amused, and a lot titillated to be hanging here crossways to his bed. He wasn't quite sure how this was supposed to work though, and he still needed to talk to Robert about the deployment...

Robert stepped back into his line of sight. He had no idea what the big man had been doing over in the corner, as the straps holding his head wouldn't allow him to tip his head back far enough to see. It was obvious Robert had been very busy in here since Christie left for work that morning. He'd built some sort of frame that fit securely onto the top of the four poster bed without damaging the antique bed. From standing it looked like a canopy bed now. It was only when the chains were attached to the edges of the frame supporting the sling in between them that it became clear Robert had turned the whole bed into a giant sex aide/restraint mechanism.

"When did you build this Robert?"

Christie's voice came out raw and breathy. God, he sounded as slutty as he felt. He couldn't tell from this angle if Robert was frowning at his question or if it was the intense look he sometimes got when he was really into what they were doing. Either one worked for him. Bossy, don't ask me any questions Robert fucked like a dream. Intense, I wanna fuck you like an animal Robert fucked like a dream. Either way Christie was screwed in the best possible way.

"Shhh, baby. Questions later."

With that Robert spanked his ass. Oh! Damn. That felt. Hot. Good. That felt like… More.

"Please!"

Robert bared his teeth at Christie. It was too feral to be a smile. If Christie's arms weren't strapped to the sling he'd have tried to reach up and touch that mouth. Robert looked like he could eat Christie up in one big bite.

"That's right baby. Beg."

Begging was not going to be a problem. Christie couldn't believe how hot it made him to be so helpless. He wanted Robert to smack his ass again.

"Robert…I…please do that again."

Christie heard a snick. Then Robert's well lubed cock was pressing against him. The big man held on to the chains by one hip.

"What do you want Christie?"

"Fucker. I want you to smack my ass again. It felt…good."

It was like flames had run from Robert's hand down into Christie's ass and then straight to his cock. Like sunshine and lightning and all the best parts of sex mixed up with a jagged edge. It felt so fucking good.

"Felt good, didn't it? Tell me again. Tell me how much you want it, baby."

Christie gritted his teeth. He wasn't going to say it again. Then Robert pulled back so that he wasn't touching Christie anywhere. Christie whimpered. He needed.

"Please Robert. It's so good. Smack my ass again… fuck me… just do something!"

Christie had squeezed his eyes shut. He needed Robert to drive the worry out of his head for a little while, take him to that place where there was no first sergeant, no deployment, just the two of them and the wicked, wicked things they did together. Laughter came from the man above him. Christie's eyes popped open, and he narrowed them at Robert, a hot wash of feeling burning into his skin like a misting of acid.

"Let me down. If I'm amusing you then obviously one of us is in the wrong place. Let me the fuck down. Now."

Christie struggled furiously, making the sling sway slightly. The straps cut into his skin where he was pulling against them, heedless of the damage he was inflicting on himself. Robert grabbed Christie's hands.

"Christie! Stop. The straps are cutting into your wrists. I wasn't laughing at you—"

"The hell you weren't."

Christie snarled and pulled harder with his arms. He managed to pull one wrist free. It had meant tearing the skin a bit, but he didn't care. He swung out with his newly freed arm.

"CHRISTIE. Stop!"

Christie froze. Robert never yelled. He blinked up at the bigger man. He'd hit Robert in the mouth. Shit. The big guy's lip was split. Double damn. Worse, there was no way he could get himself the rest of the way down without Robert's help. He winced.

"Sorry. I. Umm. Sorry. Please let me down Robert. I don't wanna be up here anymore."

Christie closed his eyes. He couldn't believe he'd hit Robert.

"I have to lower you to the bed first. Please stay still so I don't hurt you. Shit, anymore than you're already hurt. Christie, I'm sorry. I didn't think. I should have asked you for a safe word, a signal to stop everything if I did something that wasn't okay with you. I—we need to talk before we play like this again. Damn. I'm so sorry, baby."

Christie bit down on his bottom lip. Their special night was all fucked up now. He'd wanted them to have fun and get relaxed before he had to tell Robert about getting deployed. Shit.

Robert's gut clenched. He handed Christie his robe, waiting until his lover was covered. Christie would feel more secure that way. "What made you so angry? Did I scare you somehow?"

Christie plucked at the comforter for a few seconds. Then he lifted his head, looking up and holding Robert's eyes.

"You laughed at me."

Robert shook his head. He couldn't think of a single time in their entire acquaintance that he'd actually laughed at Christie. He'd certainly laughed at the way the younger man had phrased things a time or two...

Shit. The spanking.

"You thought I was laughing because you liked the spanking. Oh Christie, no wonder you tried to break my face."

In Christie's mind, there'd been a glaring occurrence of disrespect; a grievous breach of his trust. Robert bit the inside of his cheek. Shit. He felt about two inches tall.

"Forgive me for being so careless with you. I should have made sure there was no way you could feel so betrayed."

Maybe he could lighten the mood. "'Christ on a cracker'. I was thinking about your phrase and it made me laugh. I've wanted to laugh every time I've heard you say it. Is it a you are what you eat thing? Are you referring to communion somehow? I always wondered."

Christie snorted.

"It's just a phrase I picked up from my aunt. It's not like I can swear like a soldier around a kid, you know."

He cuddled close.

"I'm sorry I hit you. I was just so on edge before I got home and then you blew my mind when you sucked me off. I wasn't expecting any of that. Then the..."

Christie trailed off, gesturing at the support frame above them. Robert glanced up. He was very proud of that bit of handiwork. One day soon he and Christie were going to enjoy it to its fullest capacity. After they talked about limits. Definitely after. Tonight, however, they were going to cuddle on the bed like the most vanilla couple on the planet.

"What were you on edge about?"

Christie winced. "I found out something today at work. First sergeant said that we—the company that is—just came down on orders. It-it means we're getting deployed. Me, Robert, I'm going away. They didn't tell us for how long. Just that it would be happening within the next few weeks. He told us to make sure we get our affairs in order just—"

Robert put his hand over Christie's mouth. He didn't want to hear—wouldn't allow himself to hear those words. His baby was going away. He fought the instinct to forbid it. Christie was a grown man. As little as he liked the thought of his man going into danger he refused to treat him like a child. He looked at his hand, and slowly pulled it away, caressing the lips beneath his fingers as he did so.

"Don't say those words baby. Don't put that energy into the universe. I know it's all just busy work for the legal department, right? Because you are coming back to me, mister…and that's an order, you get me?"

Robert only realized he'd started shouting by the ache in his throat. His hands were white around Christie's shoulders in a bruising manner. He didn't want to let him go.

"Robert, I'll always come home to you. I promise. No matter what, I'll come home to you."

Robert crushed Christie against his chest. He didn't want the other man to see his eyes watering. Christie might mistake his frustration for fear, and that would never do. Two more deep breaths, and he was ready to discuss the logistics of what Christie's deployment would mean.

Robert's reaction had the fine hair on the back of Christie's neck standing on end. His mouth seemed suddenly dry, his tongue thick and unwieldy. If just hearing that he had to leave shook the big guy up this much, how were they ever going to make it through months and months of separation?

Christ on a cracker. Aunt Cate was going to shit purple polka-dotted kittens this time. She hadn't even met Robert yet, and here he was, getting ready to give the man complete power of attorney over all his affairs, to include his daughter's welfare. He should warn Robert about the likelihood she would show up in all her tie-dyed glory to interrogate him.

"Uh...you. I want you to stay here with Frankie. I could send her to my aunt you know, but I think it'll be better for her to stay here with you. Will you move in here?"

Christie held his breath. They had only been together for a little while. It was probably too soon to ask Robert for such a big commitment. Weren't engagements supposed to be long to allow for a gradual merging of lives? Christie didn't want Frankie uprooted though, not again, and he did want to be able to think of Robert here, sleeping in their bed. He wasn't sure of the logistics...would housing even allow Robert to stay here as Frankie's guardian? Would a power of attorney be enough, or should they get married before he went? He had more questions than answers at this point. He leaned back slightly so he could watch his lover's face. Robert's lips curled up at the corners and his eyes shone.

"Babe, I'd be delighted to move in with you. Even if you're not here for a while, it'll still be our place, right?"

Christie blew out the air he'd been holding. His world evened out a little. Robert wanted to live here. He still worried that the whole thing might be too much of a trial by fire, but it...gave him hope.

Part Two:
Something New

CHAPTER ELEVEN

Something old, something new
something borrowed, something blue
and a silver sixpence in his shoe.

Robert eyed the dessert cart being wheeled out of the cake decorator's back room with true antipathy. He would cheerfully vote for gouging his eyes out with Frankie's old baby spoons rather than this. He shuddered at the sight of yet another tray of cake bits being placed on the folding thing the waiter had called a "tray jack" near his table.

There was only one reason he'd felt compelled to make his upcoming wedding into a giant pain in the ass production, and that reason was currently risking his life half a world away. Christie was so excited about the whole thing he fairly wriggled all over every time they talked about their wedding in the weeks before he left.

Dammit.

Robert was so fed up with this cake tasting he wanted to bang his head on the table top. He'd worked overtime today, picking up another half-shift for Hal Byers, and then zipping straight here from work. Thank the Goddess Nikki had been able to pick Frankie up from daycare and drop her and Ally off at his house. Thankfully the whole ordeal should be over in another twenty minutes or so.

At least if Christie had been here it'd be fun. Without him, Robert was drowning in details he knew next to nothing about. How could it live up to Christie's standards?

Ring.

What was wrong with a simple hand-fasting?

Ring-ring-ring.

Christie had his heart set on a big fancy wedding. Robert didn't want to be the guy who let his partner down. Not ever.

Ring.

The last ring finally penetrated Robert's consciousness. He looked around to see if someone had left their cell phone on. Everyone in the four couples who were also participating in the "Tastes of Love" evening at the exclusive cake decorator—who Christie had picked out—were looking around. They'd all been pointedly told to turn their phones off 'in consideration for the other participants'.

The caterer seemed to recognize the ringtone, a faint frown creasing her forehead. She stepped into the entryway, picking up a phone tucked away behind what he had dubbed the 'hostess station'. A startled look crossed her face. She set the phone down and hustled over to him.

"Mr. Lindstrom? There's an urgent phone call for you."

Robert frowned up at her. Who would be calling him here?

Shit.

Ally might. His favorite niece was Frankie's sitter tonight. She had the number here.

"Alyssa? Ally-Cat? What's going on?"

The muscles in Robert's upper back clenched as if awaiting a blow. Something was wrong. Ally wouldn't have called him over something trivial.

The voice that answered wasn't Ally's.

"Mr. Lindstrom?"

"Yes, I'm Robert Lindstrom."

"This is Matt Rye; I'm a nurse here at E.J.Noble. I've got your niece Ally here, and she wants to talk to you."

"Uncle Robert?"

"Ally, honey, what's going on? Why are you at the hospital?"

"I—Frankie fell and cut her head on some glass at the park,

but I couldn't find your phone number and your cell kept going to voicemail and mom still isn't picking up—"

"Ally, are you both okay?"

"Yeah…mmm…we're okay, but Uncle Robert I didn't remember the name of the place where you are until right now and the ambulance guys had to call the police and they had to call CPS."

Robert shook his head. Ally said CPS the same way she might have said 'Freddy Krueger'. Didn't she know they were the good guys?

"Don't worry Ally. I'll be there as soon as I can, honey."

"Okay, Uncle Robert. Um, bye." Ally sniffled.

"Ally-Cat, can you be brave just a little longer? I double pinky-swear I'll be there soon."

Robert hung up the phone and walked back toward where the evening's hostess was standing. She broke off her conversation with one of the couples and met him in the middle of the room. Her expression of polite concern told him she'd picked up enough information from his side of the conversation to know he was dealing with some sort of crisis.

"Mr. Lindstrom, I gather something has come up that will prevent you from being able to stay long enough to choose your cake?"

Robert nodded his head grimly.

"My fiancé is deployed and I have guardianship of his—our daughter until he gets back. There was an accident, and I'm going to be needed at the hospital."

The hostess gave him a brisk nod and handed him her business card.

Robert glanced at it. He raised his brows in surprise. The woman hostessing tonight was the owner of Kirsten's Cakes.

"This is my direct line Mr. Lindstrom. When you're ready, we can reschedule you for another tasting at no charge to you, so you can make your decision with a clear head."

"Thanks. I appreciate that."

Robert stuck the card in his pocket. Shit. He'd have to sit through another night of eating too much cake and missing the hell out of Christie. He'd deal with that later though. He hot footed it out to his car, his heart pounding. Ally always sounded years older than she was and perfectly self assured. Tonight she sounded terribly young and scared.

Robert swung into the small parking lot at E.J.Noble over an hour later. He hadn't been able to reach Nikki at all, and the rest of the family was all in Toronto on their annual family vacation. The muscles in his neck were screaming with tension, and he'd had a horrible headache since about two minutes after he got off the phone with Ally. He just hoped she was still holding together okay.

"Shit. Where the hell is Nikki?"

Robert's nerves were jangling as he entered the ER. Having almost locked his keys in the car in his haste to get inside had cranked his building unease into painful proportions. His heart was pounding, and the throb of blood in his temples was making the headache worsen. He winced as the door to the ER's waiting room slid open. The pungent scent of antiseptic and fear that permeated every ER he'd ever been in smacked him in the face. The waiting room was mercifully fairly empty, so it only took him a moment to spot a scared looking Ally sitting next to a stern faced woman.

Who the hell was that?

Right. CPS.

The austere look on the woman's visage softened briefly as she inclined her head to better hear what Ally was saying to her. She smiled at Ally, patting her hand in a kindly fashion. Ally looked up and locked eyes with him. Robert smiled tiredly at his brave little Ally-Cat. She gestured toward him, drawing the woman's attention. The stranger said something to Ally, and then stood to met Robert part-way across the waiting room.

"Mr. Lindstrom?"

Her voice was pleasant, though a little raspy.

"Yes, and you are?"

"Stephanie Grass. I'm with the Child Protective Services."

Ms. Grass compressed her lips and heaved a tired sounding sigh.

"There was a report of an injured minor being brought in… the reporting party suspected possible neglect, as no responsible adult could be located."

Robert blinked.

Well shit.

He dropped his head forward, closing his eyes briefly, and giving in to the temptation to laugh at the absurdity of the accusation.

Ms. Grass cleared her throat.

Looking back up, he noted the dark circles under her eyes right before he locked gazes with her.

"Ms. Grass—"

"It's Mrs. Grass."

"Pardon me. Mrs. Grass, I understand how this situation might have seemed like a neglect issue…especially to a busy ER nurse or doctor. Or whoever called. I know they see far too much of that…hell, so do I. I'm a state trooper. I…"

Robert paused. The memory of Christie muttering about Frankie possibly being taken away flitted through his head. His heart clenched as he wondered how often Christie had felt that way.

"I want to check on my niece Alyssa and my fiancé's daughter first, and then I'll be happy to answer whatever questions you have for me."

Mrs. Grass gave him a measuring look. Then she pulled a card out of her purse, handing it to Robert.

"Your niece said you'd make me wait until you checked that both she and little Miss Collins were okay before you sat down to talk with me."

She broke off, looking thoughtful.

"I—honestly Mr. Lindstrom, I got called away from my daughter's spring band concert for this. I'd like to at least be there before she goes to bed tonight. Based on what you just said and my interview with your niece, I'm satisfied enough that neither child is in eminent danger to release them both into your custody. If you could call my office in the morning to schedule a home visit we can wrap up all the paper work when someone comes out to inspect your home."

Robert shook her hand bemusedly.

He really never thought he'd be on this end of a CPS investigation.

It was a damned shame so many tax dollars would be wasted on it. He watched Mrs. Grass make her way out of the ER. Out of the corner of his eye, he saw Ally launching herself at him. He turned to catch her up in his arms.

"Come on Ally-Cat. Let's go get our Frankie and go home."

CHAPTER TWELVE

"Don't freak out Christie...there was a little accident. Everybody's okay, but Frankie had to get stitches. I thought you'd want to know..."

Shit. Caro, what the hell happened?

"Simmer down, Christie. Robert was at the cake lady's tasting thingy you booked, and Ally was babysitting. You know how good she is with Frankie. Anyway, she took the baby to the park and Frankie fell on some glass. She's fine, just needed some stitches...oh, sugar... Here comes your boss."

"Specialist Collins!"

The platoon sergeant's voice sounded annoyed. Christie wondered if the man had called his name more than once, or if it was just his normal irascible nature shining through. He really hoped it was the second. If he pissed Sergeant First Class Tarans off the man could make his life miserable in ways that were too frightening to contemplate. Christie jumped up and fell into an 'at attention' position. He'd rather look like an ass than have this particular platoon daddy pissed at him.

"Oh, for fuck's sake—at ease, Specialist! Come with me. We've got an appointment at base command. Evans! Take over his spot."

After growling that out, Sergeant Tarans turned and strode angrily out of their platoon's command center. As he followed, Christie racked his brains trying to remember anything he'd done that would warrant a trip to base command headquarters.

"When we get up to headquarters, you let me do the talking. Our unit is going to be relieved early. Seems you're the first gay soldier from our battalion getting married to his partner and the publicity folks wanna make a big damned dog and pony show out of it. You have to get on the horn and let your sweetheart know to expand the guest list to include all the high brass from post as well as some of your buddies from the unit. Oh, and you'd better invite me and the lieutenant as well. At least that way you'll have two people up the chain there who actually give a shit about your wedding."

Christie gaped at Sergeant Tarans for a moment, and then blurted out the first thing that came to mind.

"But Sergeant, I thought we were still on comm blackout?"

Sergeant Tarans growled. Oh yeah, he was pissed. Thankfully it all seemed to be directed at whatever dumb-ass publicist had dreamed this shit up.

"For you, Specialist Collins, they have a secure line."

The next thing Christie knew, Sergeant Tarans had ushered him into the base commander's communication room. He waited while the communications tech on duty routed his call through. Christie wanted to call Robert's cell number to be sure he'd actually reach his lover, but the tech would only allow him to call a land line. The phone rang twice, with an echoing, distorted sound, and then Alyssa answered.

"Hello, Collins-Lindstrom residence."

Christ on a cracker, the kid was cute! He bet she'd decided on her own to hyphenate their names and to answer the phone that way. He liked the way it sounded. He'd have to talk to Robert about hyphenating their names for real once they were married.

"Ally? It's Christie. I need to talk to your Uncle Robert. Is he there?"

"Uncle Christie! I miss you so much."

Christie's heart clenched.

He quickly cleared his throat and blinked his eyes hard. He'd expected to miss Robert and Frankie when he came overseas. He hadn't expected to miss Robert's wacky family as well. He hadn't noticed how far under his skin all the Lindstroms had gotten until he was half a world away from them.

He wondered who was looking after Bergitta.

"I miss you too Ally, all of you. Will you tell everyone I said hello? Especially Bergitta."

"Um, sure Uncle Christie, if she lets me talk to her. She usually leaves when I come in the room."

The vise around Christie's heart wound a little tighter. The eyes of every administrative clerk in the room avidly watched his face.

"Ally, I really need to talk to your Uncle Robert, kiddo. Is he there?"

"No, he had to go pick mom up. Her car broke down and she left her cell in it and that's why he's not here right now."

Christie blew out a frustrated breath.

"He should be back in a few hours though. I think?"

"Hold on, Ally. I've gotta check when I can call back."

Before Christie had even finished telling Ally to hold on he could see his platoon daddy nodding at him. Okay…the brass must really be all up in arms about making his wedding into some sort of token to show their support of the GLBT bill of rights amendment. Christie wasn't sure how he felt about that.

"Ally, tell your uncle I'll call back—uh it'll be tomorrow night there—no, hold on a sec, Ally. Okay?"

"Okay Uncle Christie."

Christie looked to Sergeant Tarans. His platoon sergeant turned to the communications officer on duty.

"When should we tell Collins' family to expect his call?"

The officer flipped open the logistical folder in front of him.

"Tomorrow night, between 1700 and 1900 our time."

Christie waited for Sergeant Tarans to give him a nod. "Ally, tell your uncle I'll call the day after tomorrow at around nine in the morning, okay?"

"Okay Uncle Christie. Be safe. Come home to us soon, okay?"

"I'll do my best Ally-Cat, I'll do my best."

Christie handed the secure phone's handset back to the tech he'd gotten it from.

Sergeant Tarans nodded curtly at him, grunting for Christie to wait for him in the hallway. Christie welcomed the relative privacy afforded by stepping out of the busy communications room. He found himself vaguely reassured by the sameness of his platoon sergeant's manner.

"I'll bring Specialist Collins back in tomorrow evening."

Christie found himself hustled back out of the base's command center. Once they were outside striding past the chow hall, Sergeant Tarans seemed to relax down from the high-alert 'I wanna plant my size fourteen boots firmly in your ass' tenseness he'd been broadcasting in the communications room.

"I didn't think they needed to butt into any more of your family's business. Shouldn't be any of Command's business unless you make it their business."

Christ on a cracker with cheddar and jalapeños! Christie was hard put to not let his jaw drop open. He knew he hadn't succeeded when the old man barked out a laugh, and clapped him on the shoulder hard enough to nearly knock him over.

They walked back toward their platoon's command tent. Sergeant Tarans scoured the area with his steely gaze.

"Private Johnson-relieve Evans for chow."

Christie saw Evans jump up through the open tent flap. He hotfooted it over to Christie's side. Their platoon sergeant waved them both off abruptly.

"Evans, Collins, report back to me after chow."

Evans and Christie hurried to make it before the dfac closed. The chow line was short, but seemed to be moving especially slow. Christie shrugged his shoulders, content to wait in silence. He could use the time to prepare himself for his call to Robert. Christie hated having to talk to Robert in front of everyone up at Base Command. There was so much he wanted to say, but he'd sooner low crawl the length of the motorpool, dragging his belly over broken glass, than embarrass himself and Sergeant Tarans in front of the base command non-commissioned officers tomorrow evening. As he got to an empty table he realized he'd forgotten to stop by the condiment table to doctor up his eggs.

Christie set his breakfast tray down on the table.

"Evans, grab a Tabasco bottle and bring it back with you."

A blast rocked the dfac. It had to be close by, if they could feel it in the dining facility right as it happened. Evans stumbled as he turned around. His mouth was moving but the ringing in Christie's ears made it impossible to hear what he was saying.

Shit.

That had to be the mailroom, or the gym.

Christie knew Jenkins was on duty this morning in the mailroom. Sergeant Richards would be in the gym. Fuck. Either way he lost a friend today.

A hand clamped down on his upper arm, strong fingers digging into the bicep, forcing him to still. Christie hadn't realized he was running for the door until he jerked to a stop. Evans mouth moved quickly, but the faint sound was drowned out by the ringing in Christie's ears.

The ringing was outside his head. Alarms.

Evans brought his free hand up next to his own face in a fist.

Right. That was the hand-signal to stop.

Then he shook Christie's arm, hard.

Releasing the smaller man, Evan's brought both arms up parallel to the floor, hands balled into fists, bent them at the elbows, and touched both shoulders.

Fuck. Gas Mask. Last thing he needed now was a lung full of anthrax or a blister agent.

Christie grabbed the flap of case resting on his right hip, flipped it up, and pulled his mask out, securing it against his face. The soft rubber molded to his face, letting him know his seal was good. As he tightened the head straps down to keep it in place,

Christie wondered what the fuck he'd do if Evans didn't have his back.

Evans secured his mask then looked to Christie for direction.

Christie made for the door.

At the door to the dfac as he paused for Evans to catch up, Christie checked the straps holding his mask to his head once more, and jerked the sleeves of his BDU jacket down, buttoning them at the wrists. The rough feel of the material against his skin was comforting. It meant the specially treated fabric would be between his skin and whatever chemical threat might be out there.

He watched Evans dip into the kitchen area to grab their emergency medical kit off the shelf over the prep area. One of the cooks was yelling at Evans. It looked like the explosion had knocked a big pot of something onto a couple of the kitchen workers. Evans pulled something out of the kit and tossed it to the man yelling at him.

It figured Evans would know where the med kit was. Christie knew where his unit's was, because he and Evans had just finished Combat Lifesaver training two weeks ago. Evans was the original doom and gloom guy though, figuring he needed to know where every kit on the base was, or at least all the ones in places he frequented.

Turned out he was right.

Evans sidled up next to him, pantomiming holding a weapon. Christie knew just what he was saying. He wished they had their M16's, too.

Christie nodded. He drew in a deep breath to try to slow his racing heart. Yeah. Having his weapon in hand would feel a lot better than going out armed with nothing but a half-assed medical kit.

Evans indicated he would take the high position going out the door, so Christie took low. There was no real reason to, not without their weapons. Christie knew that, but it still felt better than just running out blind.

One step out the door and he could see the MP's down the hill from them directing folks away.

Two steps out the door he could see it had been the mail room.

The metal side of the gym's wall was bent in, and Sergeant Richards was sitting on the ground in the doorway, blood running thick and dark red down one side of his face.

Shit.

Evans gestured to himself, Richards, and then back to Christie. He'd get Richards checked out and then be right over to help Christie check for survivors.

Christie shook his head. The alarms went silent. Christie could still see them flashing. He leaned in close.

"No, Evans. You should stay with Sergeant Richards. The medics will be up here as soon as the MP's clear them to come up. You get him down to the hospital. I'll have plenty of help in a minute or two."

Evans bumped fists with him. Thank fuck he'd heard that.

"Stay safe, Collins."

Christie could see the 89Deltas crawling all over the twisted heap of metal that had been the mailroom already. Those bomb squad guys were fucking fearless, crazy, or both. One of them gave the all clear sign, and they all ripped off their masks.

Christie took his off as well, and then wished he hadn't.

The air smelled like a barbeque restaurant, heavy on the charcoal. Christie gagged a little. He could taste a hint of burnt meat in the air.

But if the bomb guys were over there he could at least go in and see if he could help…anyone. The MP's probably wouldn't let anyone up the hill until the bomb guys gave the all clear for ordinance. If anyone—fuck, man, Jenkins had kids—in the mailroom had survived…well they might not make it until the medics got cleared to come up.

Christie strode toward the heap of metal that had been the mailroom. One of the bomb guys made to stop him. Christie held up the emergency med kit.

"Combat Lifesaver trained."

The guy nodded. His eyes looked bleak.

"We can maybe use you. Our Combat Lifesaver guy is Stateside. Emergency leave. Stay over by the gym. There's just… pieces…so far, but maybe we'll find someone still whole, and breathing. If we do, we'll bring them to you."

Christie waited in the hot sun, watching the smears of Sergeant Richards' blood drying to a rusty brown color in the gym's doorway. Time seemed to be working wrong. Though twenty long minutes passed, it felt like one slow beat of time, just a blink. Christie knew the sun was beating against him, but he felt chilled to the bone. His ears still rang, but now he could hear whispers behind the screaming silence.

The 89Delta he'd spoken to before came over, smears of soot and something clumpy and grey on his uniform pants.

"None of them made it. Fucking mess over there."

Christie swallowed hard. He was pretty sure he had a good idea what those grey clumps were. He nodded numbly.

Fuck.

Jenkins had just shown Christie a picture of his new baby last week. Christie bit the inside of his cheek until he tasted a hot coppery flavor. Then he walked back to the dfac, turning the emergency med kit back over to the still stunned cooks.

He went looking for Evans, Sergeant Tarans, and the ass-chewing he knew was coming.

Fuck. He'd be lucky if Sergeant Tarans didn't slap an article fifteen on him for what he'd done. He and Evans might be the same rank, but he'd had his for six months longer, and so was technically higher ranking. Christie knew his platoon sergeant would see it that way. Sergeant Tarans would have expected them to stay in the dfac until the 89Deltas cleared the site. Then he would have expected them to report back to him immediately and let the medics handle any injuries.

"Well, Collins, Evans. Since you've already volunteered in this affair, I guess you won't mind helping the mail clerks out with the clean-up, will you?"

The old man had gone one better than the worst Christie had been able to dream up on his own. Christie sucked up his horror at just what the corrective action was going to be. At this point, he was just thankful there weren't actual charges placed against him.

Dammit.

The Army was so screwed up sometimes. He knew he'd done the right thing.

And Sergeant Tarans knew he'd done the wrong thing.

Double Fuck.

Sergeant Tarans always said how much he hated his soldiers putting themselves in what he termed 'unnecessary danger'. It was one of the old man's hot buttons, so he made sure every soldier who came into his platoon got the 'unnecessary danger' lecture.

Christie wouldn't have changed anything he did this morning, but he knew better than to piss Sergeant Tarans off any more.

"Roger that, Sergeant Tarans. When do we report?" He'd rather they 'volunteer' to clean up the debris from the bomb blast than have Evans come out with one of his patented smart-ass comments and land them in even more trouble.

CHAPTER THIRTEEN

Sergeant Tarans sent Johnson up to relive Evans after a couple of hours. He was there for most of the heavy lifting stuff, but was gone before they got to the part where they were trying to decide which body parts went in which pile. Christie was fiercely glad. Shit, he didn't want to be here, up to his elbows in twisted metal and what he thought might be Jenkins's thigh.

Fuck.

Evans was tough…but Christie sensed an unseen hurt in his friend that wouldn't have stood up to this.

So.

Best he was monitoring the command tent again.

The dfac brought MRE's out for them around lunch, but really? Christie couldn't have eaten one of those ready to eat meals if he'd been given a direct order to at that point. The thick smell of overcooked meat still lingered in the air, and he didn't know if he'd ever get the image of Jenkins's half blown away head out of his head.

He took two of the cold waters they were passing around and grimly went back to separating scrap metal from blown to shit mail from chunks of what used to be people as sweat trickled down between his shoulder blades.

Hell, he was even qualified for this. Had his hazmat certification and everything.

Six hours later the worst of the mess was set to rights. The coroners had come and taken all the body parts. The thick burnt meat smell went with them, or at least enough of it for Christie to choke down an apple after the sergeant in charge of the clean up dismissed them for the day.

He washed his hands and face, grabbed the apple, and headed back to release Evans for chow. He was too numb to be anything but relived that the worst part of the clean up was done.

Sergeant Tarans wasn't in the command tent when Christie got there, but Evans was.

"Hey Evans, I can take over the monitoring again."

Evans shook his head and continued reading the latest Ethan Day novel, the one Evans had teased him about having on his e-reader. "No can do Collins. Sergeant Tarans will hand me my nuts pureed in a bitty glass jar if I let you take over right now. He called down from the base dfac and said exactly that. He also said you were to stay put right here until he gets back, and I was to remain at my post."

Fuck.

Sergeant Tarans hadn't said he could go to chow.

He'd told him to report back after he got released.

Christie prepared himself for another ass-reaming.

Evans shifted in his seat, completely absorbed in his reading.

Damn. Judging by the pup-tent Evans was pitching over there, getting the book next was worth whatever he asked for it.

Christie bet it might even take his mind off what he'd seen today.

Well.

It might.

And seriously, that was worth almost anything.

He eyed Evans's surprisingly large erection, straining in his pants.

He really wished he was home with Robert, getting his woefully-neglected-because-of-deployment ass fucked through the mattress. He knew for a fact that would get him out of his head long enough to relax.

"Remember you're getting married soon, oh slutty one!"

Christie jumped in surprise, and then shrugged at Evans when the man raised his head from his book to look up at him.

Evans's cheeks were faintly pink.

Huh.

It was a good look on him.

"Jay-zus, you're still easier to spread than Jiffy's extra-creamy aren't you?"

Christ on a cracker, Caro! Just because I noticed his—sizeable—endowments doesn't mean I'm going to take him through a crash course of Gay Sex 101. And stop damn popping in on me like that. Announce yourself like normal people.

"Uh...announce myself like normal people? Christie, just how many dead people do you talk to?"

Christie ignored her. It was far more entertaining to guess how high Evans's pup tent was gonna rise. The pink in his cheeks was spreading down his neck now.

He could hear Caro sniffing at him.

What? Like you never thought about anybody but Liss.

How Caro made silence sound like a delicate sniff of disbelief ranked right up there with the mystery of what the Mona Lisa model had been smiling about, and why the smile was so...creepy.

Caro had been able to do that silent delicate disapproval thing when she was alive. It really wasn't fair she could still do it after death.

Christie peeked at the gorgeous bulge—and, oh it really had been too long since he'd seen Robert. He jumped up and headed for the entrance to the tent before he did something crazy like fall to his knees to offer Evans his first blowjob from a man.

"Uh, I'm just gonna wait for Sergeant Tarans outside." He bolted out of the tent.

He'd been mesmerized.

It made perfect sense.

Snakes that strangled their prey hypnotized them with their eyes before they devoured them, right?

Well, there you had it. He'd been mesmerized by that damned one-eyed python Evans was packing.

Holy shit, Caro; I think you just saved me from getting divorced.

"You're not married yet Christie."

Yeah Caro, I know, but I wouldn't have told him about that and risked losing him… I'd wait until you told him, and then I'd beg for forgiveness. You know it's easier to get that after the fact than it is to get permission before.

"You'd have left without me anyway, Christie. The only one you're slutty for these days is Robert. Shocked the hell out of me when that happened, but it did."

Caro…you do know you're a really bad liar, right? You just got done saying I spread easier than extra-creamy peanut butter…and I know you think Robert's the best thing to ever happen to me. So you can stop pretending you're not scared spitless I'm gonna fuck this up.

"Shit."

Yeah. Don't feel bad Caro. I'm scared too.

Sergeant Tarans ambled to a stop in front of the tent. His smile was the single most frightening thing Christie had ever seen, grim and twisty with nicotine stains. Sergeant Tarans was a great Platoon sergeant, he was a highly skilled tactician, and he was the most unscrupulous fighter Christie had ever met. It did not bode well to have Sgt. Tarans smile at one. Crap. It was time to take his punishment for disobeying Sergeant Tarans again.

"Specialist Collins, I'm so glad to see you out here. I've been meaning to find someone with a little free time to police up this area in front of our platoon's tents."

Christie looked down the row of tents. Every single one had a disgusting amount of litter around the coffee cans they'd all scavenged from the mess-hall to use as impromptu trash cans/butt cans for their stubbed out cigarettes and scraps of candy wrappers. Sergeant Tarans was giving him the look; the one that said, 'please give me a reason to ream you out a little harder soldier'.

"Roger that, Sergeant. I'm your guy. Got nothing but time on my hands today."

Sergeant Tarans grinned at him tightly. Christie could tell the old man was enjoying this. Grumbling under his breath once Sergeant Tarans went in to the unit's command tent, Christie set about his disgusting task. He was surprised when Specialist Evans came hot-footing it out of the tent less than a minute after the platoon sergeant went in. Evans made a bee-line for him.

Please don't let Evans be coming to work with him.

Christie held his breath, and let his eyelids fall mostly shut. If willpower alone were enough to pull it off, Evans would already be reassigned to work with Second Platoon. They were over two hundred miles away. That was probably far enough away to keep Christie out of trouble.

He was itchy, like his skin didn't fit right, and his brain kept circling from an image of the empty inside of Jenkins's skull to the idea of how much he really needed…something to make him feel alive right now. A fight. A fuck.

Anything that could make him feel less off-kilter.

Evans stopped right in front of him. He eyed Christie up like an alley cat eyes up the scraps thrown out behind the fishmonger's shop.

Christie didn't care what Evans said, there was not a single chance on the planet he was one hundred percent straight. The fact he was raised by a queer couple might make him sensitive to the challenges a gay guy faced even in today's more liberal military. It might even make him more likely to flirt a little, just out of common courtesy and good manners. It would not make him look at his buddy like he'd been three days in the scorching desert and said buddy was an ice cold glass of lemonade.

Interesting.

"Sgt. Tarans sent me to help you."

Evans looked mightily pissed.

Well, pissed and horny.

Christie shot a glance at Evans's right side cargo pocket. No bulge from his e-reader. Sergeant Tarans must have busted him for forgetting to have the wi-fi feature disabled again. Christie deliberately smirked at his friend in the most smart-assed manner he could achieve.

"Old man wanted your e-reader, huh?"

Evans grunted and nodded sourly. Christie couldn't stop the laugh bubbling up out of him at Evans's expression. He'd felt the same way during their last training deployment when the old man had told him he was starting to worry about Christie's fitness... right after Christie got a care package from his Aunt Cate full of home baked cookies. The old fraud had just wanted half the cookies.

"You should never have loaned him that paperback anthology with Sno-Ho in it. You'll be lucky if he ever lets you have your reader back."

Christie and Evans both cracked up at that. Who knew crusty old Sergeant Tarans would turn out to be an avid romance reader? After a minute, they turned to look up the row of tents at all the work they had to do. Evans sighed.

"You think if we yell out Rumpietiltskin some horny little dude with bad hair will come and do it for us?"

Christie rolled his eyes. "Rump-el-stiltskin, moron! Geez! And even if he did, I'm not giving up my first born or my fine ass to get this mess cleaned up."

Now Evans made a point checking out Christie's ass. He then looked with exaggerated horror at the butts on the ground before throwing one hand up to his chest and thrusting out a hip.

"Oh sugar." Evan's falsetto was so high it should have cracked glass. "It's only fair you give the little dude some fine ass for cleaning up all the foul butts for us."

They stood silent as a moment creaked by; Christie gaping at Evans and Evans blinking back at him in patently phony innocence. Then they fell into each other, laughing like a pair of demented hyenas.

Sergeant Tarans growled at them from inside the tent. "Get

to work you lazy little shits, and keep the noise level down. I'm at a good par—I'm busy with work in here!"

Mouthing the words 'good part' to one another, they moved up the row, still snickering, and started cleaning up the stubbed out cigarettes. Sergeant Tarans wasn't an asshole, so after about an hour five more platoon members who'd managed to piss him off somehow in the last day or two got sent out to help them. With the additional help, they were done in time to make it to the beer tent while they still had some decent beer. Better yet, Evans was friends with one of the servers, so they didn't have to spend much time waiting for their beers. She even slipped them some extras. After his fourth beer, Christie thought a little blearily he should have probably had something more than one small apple to eat before they started drinking.

Oh well.

And if he'd pissed Caro off after the third beer, telling her to fuck off when she tried to get him to slow down? Well, at least it was getting harder to remember the visuals from earlier today clearly. He belched loudly and then chuckled. Good ole' Evans brought him another beer right on cue. It was turning out to not be such a bad night after all.

CHAPTER FOURTEEN

Later Christie found himself flat on his back in the front of his truck, sprawled across the bench seat with Evan's hands on the buttons of his pants and the man's tongue in his mouth. The man had a truly talented tongue. Christie reeled a little internally at the hot, perfect strokes of Evans's tongue against his. There was a moment of triumphant aha-ness at this irrefutable proof of Evans's not so straight tendencies.

It kicked the shit out of his Jenkins-vision, shut off the instaplay of the man's half empty skull, and made Christie feel alive.

For a few minutes he could even pretend it was okay.

Then an image of Robert; laughing as he shot Christie at Lasertron, his teeth glowing in the black light flashed in his mind.

The Oh Shit Choir kicked in with their special version of the Hallelujah Chorus. He twisted his head to one side.

"Evans…Evans, I'm sorry man. I can't. I just can't."

Evans ignored him, grabbing Christie's chin and twisting it back to bring his lips back in range. The bigger man kissed him with a breath-stealing intensity, as though there were only the two of them in all the world and they had a limitless time to lay exploring one another's mouths. Then Evans ground down against him. Their cocks slid against each other. The feel of the bigger man's naked flesh sliding against his own nearly had Christie losing track of what he meant to say. It felt terrifyingly good.

And when the hell did he get their pants open? Christie was sure his were still closed when he told Evans to stop. Then Evans had kissed him again and… he didn't remember the next bit.

Shit.

He couldn't do this.

His image of Robert pushed back the drive to let his stupid cock lead the rest of his body merrily down a path Christie knew would make him hate himself.

"I can't do this Evans. Stop. I'm getting married when I get home."

Evans grunted, pulling his lips off Christie's neck momentarily. He slid open mouthed kisses back along Christie's jaw until he reached the hollow below his ear, nipping the earlobe there.

"You're not married yet." That whispered rasp was the sort of thing that usually made Christie's blood burn, but the echo of Caro's words totally had Christie's hands clenching into fists. If he couldn't fuck Evans he could still fight him. He pushed Evans to one side, causing the bigger man to slide partway off the seat.

He drew back his arm, balling up his fist. A flash of hurt chased across Evans's handsome face. A flash of white blanked out Christie's vision for a moment. His jaws clenched together as the taste of bile rippled into Christie's mouth. He eyed the distance between his hand and Evans' face. His gut clenched.

Shit.

He couldn't hit his friend. The poor guy's eyes were getting big and shocky, looking into the phantom distance as Evans shivered beside him. Christie got it. He felt as jagged as the scraps of metal from the mailroom too.

"I know Evans. I was—I need just as much as you do right now. So yeah, my stupid cock might just love what you were doing, and for sure my ass seems to lack any sort of morals and would love to have your big cock up it. But I love Robert, and this would hurt him. I'm sorry. I didn't mean to tease. I like you Evans, and if there wasn't Robert, I'd already have my legs up for you…but—"

Evans smiled. It was a little too tight and brittle at the edges. Still, it was a smile.

"Yeah, I get it Collins. I-I'm sorry too, man. That I didn't stop when you asked the first time. I like you Collins. You know? And I just wanted…I wanted to feel alive, you know?"

Christie had to look away then.

Yeah.

He got it. That was how he'd ended up here.

Evans's eyes were so intent they almost glowed. Looking down reminded Christie he was sitting there with his pants pulled open and his humiliatingly still hard cock wagging out in the open. He hastily pulled them closed, adjusting his traitorous flesh so that he could button them shut. His stomach hurt like he'd eaten a bowl full of suicide hot wings, and his chest was dangerously tight.

"I'm really sorry Evans. I—I gotta go man."

Christie pulled the latch on the door behind him, half falling, half crawling out of the big truck's cab. He ended up on his ass next to the front tires, looking up at Evans's pale, shocked face peering out of the truck's cab.

"Collins, wait a minute. You're really hammered man…let me help you back to the tent at least, so you don't get in trouble with the MP's or run into Sergeant Tarans while you're all fucked up. The old man's already pissed enough at you."

Christie didn't stop. He scrambled to his feet, and then turned and sprinted out of the motorpool. He kept running all the way through the encampment, ignoring the looks his odd behavior drew, only stopping when he reached the little curtained off cubicle that housed his bunk. He stripped out of his dirty uniform and scrubbed at his skin with a handful of baby wipes. They reminded him of Frankie, making him feel even more like hammered shit. He pulled on the shorts and tee-shirt he slept in and curled into a ball under his covers.

He was still lying there awake when Evans made it back to the tent nearly three hours later. Evans sounded drunker than he'd been before, and downright miserable when he slurred Christie's name softly through the curtain. Christie closed his eyes and evened out his breathing until he heard Evans's footsteps move away. When he was sure the other man was gone, he opened his eyes again. He lay like that a while longer, fighting to keep his breathing quiet as tears slipped silently down his face.

Robert deserved a better man than this.

A strong scent of Obsession perfume permeated the tent that night. Breathing it in, on top of his already spinning head came close to making Christie vomit.

He managed, barely, to keep his stomach contents down.

He couldn't get warm, not even when he put his sweatpants and hoodie on. The space along his back where Robert's chest and stomach would press as he curled into Christie was achingly cold. The space in his arms where Frankie's little sleep-sweet body would fit echoed with emptiness. Lying there in his bunk he shivered, pulled the pillow from under his head to hug tightly, and wished like hell he were home.

He listened carefully, and even called out for her mentally, but Caro's voice didn't sound in his head at all that night. He wasn't surprised. Obsession had always been the scent of her disapproval when she was alive.

Christie swatted at the hand shaking his shoulder. It was too damned early to be getting up on a weekend. Robert must have gotten one of his crazy notions that he could make Christie a morning person by sheer dint of will.

"Lemme be Nalle…"

The hand shook him again, harder.

"Dammit Robert, stoppit or I'll teach Frankie to call you Nalle too. Then you'll be stuck being called Teddy Bear forever… lemme sleep…"

A low chuckle sounded above him. That wasn't Robert's voice. Christie's eyes popped open to the sight of Evans holding out a bottle of juice and a travel sized bottle of ibuprofen. A faintly wistful expression marked his face.

"Geez Collins, you really do have it bad, don't you? You can't even imagine anyone else touching you."

Christie reached out and took the peace offering Evans had brought. The guy definitely had a flare for picking out which gifts to grovel with. Nothing in the whole freaking camp could have been more welcome right at that moment than the painkillers. Christie's head throbbed to a marching band drum section warming up inside it.

"No Evans, I really can't. Robert's the only guy for me."

Christie swallowed two of the extra-strength tablets down as he checked the time on his wrist watch. Twenty-five minutes until first formation. He should start feeling human before he had to run thanks to Evans's timely pain med intervention.

"Thanks for the ranger candy, Evans."

The surprised laugh that got from Evans was worth the effort of talking civilly before he had caffeine. Christie wanted coffee so badly he could swear he smelled it. It figured his crazy brain would conjure up the smell to tantalize him.

"Christ on a cracker, I'd kill for a hot cuppa joe."

Evans grinned. He looked like a little kid bringing soggy toast and a mauled carnation to his mom's bedroom on mother's day. Then he reached behind himself and produced a ceramic dining facility mug from the top of Christie's make-shift desk.

"No need to kill, compadre."

Christie gaped at him. Then he held his hands out, opening and closing them in the classic 'gimme-gimme' motion. Evans handed over the cup. Christie slurped down a wonderfully burning mouthful of coffee.

"I think I love you, man."

Christie froze the second the words left his mouth. Evans choked on his own mouthful of coffee, taken from a second cup which Christie hadn't noticed until then. Christie squeezed his eyes shut. Evans sputtered, coughed, and then started laughing.

"Geez Collins, awk-waaard!"

Just that simply they were pals again, both laughing at their mutual love of the brilliant tongue-in-cheek by-play of nearly every bit of dialogue in the latest cartoon remake of Little Red Riding Hood. Christie laughed until his eyes were watering. He looked up at Evans as he wiped the laughter tears out of his eyes.

"We okay now?"

Evans nodded seriously. The corner of his mouth was still quirked up in amusement, but the steady gaze he trained on Christie said that he'd heard the question and understood all it meant. He tapped his wrist watch as he polished off the last of his coffee.

"Better get your lazy ass outta bed there, princess, or Sergeant Tarans will rip you a new one, again, this time for being late to physical training."

Christie smiled at his friend. He took another swallow of his shitty coffee, thankful Evans had remembered how sweet he liked it. Then he swung his legs out of bed, stood, and swallowed the last of the blissfully caffeinated beverage before following Evans out of the tent.

CHAPTER FIFTEEN

That evening on the way up to Base Command's communication center, Christie remembered what he'd meant to tell his platoon sergeant before the mail room incident.

"Sergeant Tarans, I already had you and the lieutenant on the list of people to invite. I-I didn't know if you could come, because of the rules about fraternizing, but I wanted you both to know I wanted you there."

Sergeant Tarans gave one of his characteristic grunts in acknowledgement.

"We'll be there Collins. Someone's gotta keep the brass from turning your wedding into a complete goat-fuck."

Christie took a deep breath. His eyes stung. Trust the crusty old bastard to figure out a way to tell you he loved you like a son without ever saying the words.

Robert waited by the phone in a state of fierce anticipation. It had been three months since he'd heard his lover's voice. Christie had warned him that they would likely be under a communication blackout for at least the first few months, possibly longer. The reality of it had been much harder than Robert had anticipated. There had been so many nights when he'd just ached to hear Christie say anything. He hadn't changed the outgoing message on the home phone…some nights he'd turn the ringer's off on all the house phones so he wouldn't wake Frankie, and he'd call the number over and over just to hear Christie say they weren't home.

Ring.

Ri—

Robert snatched the phone up before the second ring finished. He held his breath as he waited for the person on the other end of the phone to speak. When Christie's sweetly husky tenor came across the line he nearly wept with relief.

"Hello… Robert, are you there?"

Robert smacked himself on the forehead as he answered. The person answering the phone usually spoke first.

"Christie. It's good to hear your voice, babe."

He swallowed hard against the emotions filling his throat. He—Christie was in a dangerous place, and he wanted to support him, not leave him feeling like things were falling apart back home.

"Is the communication blackout over for good now babe? I know Frankie misses you something awful and it'll be great if—"

Robert's throat closed off like he'd taken too big a bite and swallowed without chewing.

"I miss you babe. I miss you so damn much. It's harder than I thought, doing this without you."

There was a weird silence, and then his own voice echoed back the last thing he'd said. He waited anxiously for the bizarre ricochet of sound to finish.

"Oh, Robert, I miss you too. We're still in blackout officially… but the brass want to make sure our wedding plans are running smoothly. I guess they want to publically support the first same-sex wedding in the battalion; us. I… I know you weren't wild about the whole overdone wedding spectacle thing …but I'm afraid it's about to get a lot bigger."

Christie's voice carried a wince that made Robert smile despite himself. Yeah, he hated the ridiculous, expensive hoopla that their wedding was becoming, but it was worth suffering through to make Christie happy.

"I don't mind Christie. I'd like us to have a little private ceremony at some point, though."

Laughter rippled over the line, mixing with the echo of his own words. It disoriented him for a moment. He closed his eyes and breathed against the sensation of dislocation, but that only made it worse. For just a second he could smell Christie's subtly spicy scent mixed with a hot dry odor he'd never smelled before. He smiled to himself.

"I told you to pack more deodorant Christie."

Christie sucked in a sharp breath.

"I know Robert; I should have listened to you. I have good news, though." Christie spoke quickly, as though trying to stop Robert from saying any more.

"I'll be home to help with some of the planning of the wedding for sure."

Robert swallowed against the tightness in his throat.

"Well, will we be able to at least write you soon? I went to a family readiness group meeting and they were explaining that we need to mail boxes out for Christmas as soon as we get your address or you might not get the stuff in time…do you know when they're lifting the blackout, babe?"

There was a long pause. Only the metallic echo told Robert he was still connected to the line. "I can't say exactly when. I love you. Give Frankie kisses from me. I. I miss you so damn much-"Christie's voice cracked hard enough to make Robert wince.

Then there was a sharp noise, as if the phone had been dropped suddenly against a hard surface.

"Mr. Lindstrom, this is Sergeant Tarans." Well, that older, rougher, deeper voice certainly wasn't Christie's. "I'm Collin's platoon sergeant. He had to step away from the phone. I'm sorry, but we can't wait for him to get back. He'll be able to call you again soon. Someone from publicity there at headquarters will be coming out to the house to bring you a list of the folks from his chain of command who would like to attend the wedding."

An irritated sounding snort came through the static filled connection.

"It's important for his career that you make sure those names get included, son. You needn't worry about mailing my invite; you can put me down as a yes plus one. I have to sign off now. I look forward to meeting you."

The echoing noise came back, but nothing followed it. Robert hung the phone up. He sat silently in the living room for close to an hour after that. Staring through the patio doors to the place where he'd first kissed Christie.

He hated the not knowing if Christie was okay, and all the empty space between them. He needed his man to come home in one piece.

Christie couldn't believe he'd almost lost it in front of everyone in the communications room. He'd tried to tell Robert about the thing with Evans. It was just too hard to talk about standing in the close cement room with all those other guys in hearing range. The one clerk was so close Christie could smell his Old Spice deodorant. It smelled just like Evans had when—

He wasn't going to think about that. Or the way Jenkins had always worn the same damned cheap stuff.

God help him if they ever found out his Aunt Cate was a famous psychic and that his boyfriend—fiancé could tell what he smelled like from half a world away, or that his dead best friend talked to him in his head. Right. Hello, rubber room.

He made his way back to his unit command post, knowing Sergeant Tarans would find him there. He'd take the ass-chewing he knew was coming for taking off again. Christie stepped back into the air-conditioned tent that housed his unit's command post and addressed the soldier who'd covered for him.

When Sergeant Tarans got back, though he gave Christie an evil glare, he just grunted at him and told him to go find Simmons to take over monitoring the command tent.

CHAPTER SIXTEEN

Robert woke the next morning to find Frankie snuggled up to him. He dredged through his memories and came up with a vague recollection of picking her up out of her toddler bed in the middle of the night. The pain medicine he'd given her before bed had worn off, and even when the new dose kicked in she'd been restless and fretful. So he'd brought her into his and Christie's room to lay with him. He turned his head to watch Frankie breathing in her sleep.

There was so much of Christie in his daughter. The shape of their foreheads and noses was the same. So was the shape of their eyes, and the way their top lips were fuller than their lower lips. Frankie's hair was solidly black though, so dark she looked like a comic book heroine.

Robert had never seen such coloring on another living person. Christie said she looked just like her mother. Robert had never seen a picture of Caro. There didn't seem to be any in the house. The one time Robert had asked about it, Christie said he couldn't have them in the house. It had been worded oddly, as though Christie was implying that some force outside of himself wouldn't allow the pictures.

"Well, sweet girl, why don't we try to find some pictures of your mom for you? I bet Christie would like to have some pictures of his best friend as well."

Robert shook his head at himself. Nikki had tried to warn him that single parenting would quickly have him talking to himself and acting even goofier than he normally did. He'd scoffed at her. He was so going to have to pay up on that bet. He scooted out of bed. He didn't know how Christie did it. He was lucky to get a shower on the days he had to go in to work before daycare opened.

If he was lucky, Gran would be able to watch her. He'd call his brother Christoffer later that evening. It wouldn't hurt to ask if he could be counted on to drive Gran over or pick her up depending on Robert's schedule.

Single parenthood without any discernible support system sucked. Robert had an up close and personal tour of that last night. That Christie'd managed to cope so well for the time before he'd left for deployment was a testament to the man's inner strength. Robert wasn't sure he could have coped. Hell, he could barely cope with his extensive and extremely helpful family's full support.

Something Nikki had been doing without.

Oh, sure, she took some assistance here and there…but for the most part she'd been as alone as Christie. Except in Nikki's case, it had been for the past eleven years. And no one in their family had noticed. She hardly ever asked for help, and when she did, it was in such an offhand way it never seemed urgent. It never seemed like something she really needed. Robert couldn't help but wonder if he and the rest of the family had somehow made her feel as if she shouldn't ask for help.

Yet another phone call he'd need to make tonight. This year he was going to offer to take Ally during his vacation time before she had to ask. It was the least he could do. He decided to risk trying to get Frankie back in her own bed. He really needed a shower. He smelled like a combination of stale cake, panic-sweat, and emergency waiting room.

Robert ended up calling in to work. The daycare needed a note from her pediatrician to accept Frankie into care with her stitches, as well as another giving them both permission to and explicit instructions for how to give both the painkiller and the antibiotic the emergency room doctor had prescribed. Now he needed to call Frankie's pediatrician to get those forms filled out so he could go to work tomorrow.

More telephone time. Joy.

After twenty-five minutes of annoying, automated answering systems, Robert finally got through. Truthfully it was partly his fault. He kept getting so frustrated he'd hang up and try dialing again, despite the repeated warnings that calls were taken in the order that they were received.

He was ready to weep with joy when he discovered the magic number combination to put his call through to an actual person and managed to hold on to his patience long enough to wait out the four callers ahead of him.

It didn't matter that the person was cranky, suspicious of his right to make medical decisions for Frankie, and reluctant to book him into a same day appointment.

"Sir, the walk in clinic hours here at Primrose Pediatrics are from seven am to nine am. I'm afraid you've already missed those hours for today."

Robert gritted his teeth. "This isn't a routine sick visit."

Robert made certain to speak slowly and surely; it was the only way to keep his growing irritation out of his voice. "It's a follow-up appointment to an emergency room visit."

"You don't need to shout at me, sir." Robert resisted the urge to stare incredulously at the phone for that offended tone. Barely. "I didn't realize it was for a follow-up to an ER visit. Hold please."

Robert ground his teeth together again to keep down the growl building at the back of his throat. At this rate, he was going to need an appointment with a dentist too.

"Well ma'am, I've no idea why you wouldn't have heard it before. It was the first thing I said to you, and I've said it at least four or five times since then. The last time I checked I sounded nothing like the teacher from Charlie Brown's school, so I really couldn't say why you didn't hear what I was saying…unless of course, you weren't actually listening."

There was a long, empty silence.

"We have an opening at eleven-fifteen. Can you make that?"

Robert smiled to himself. The woman sounded both pissed and impressed. "Eleven-fifteen will be fine. Where are you located?"

He jotted down the address, said a polite and totally undeserved thank you, and hung up. Screw giving Christie a hug and a big kiss when he got home; Robert was going to buy him a spa-package with at least six full body massages included.

Not to get back in his good graces for letting Frankie get hurt while he was gone. He wanted Christie to have it as an 'I'm sorry I didn't realize what a huge task parenting is and help out more' present.

Okay, it would also serve the sucking up to get back in Christie's good graces purpose…once he actually told him about Frankie's accident. He might not even need a sucking up present once he explained to Christie why he waited to tell him.

Hopefully.

When the doctor walked into the exam room Robert almost swallowed his tongue. This was not the sweet little blonde woman Christie had told him about the last time he'd taken Frankie in for shots. This doc was easily six feet, two inches of sex on legs. He had amber eyes fringed with long, thick, curly black lashes. They were slightly almond shaped and set above high cheekbones framing beautiful bronze skin.

Damn, but he missed Christie. It had been too long.

"Ba-ba!"

Robert looked down at Frankie in surprise. Her little hands were lifted up, grasping at the doc's stethoscope. There was indeed a battered elephant wearing a crown and a green suit wrapped around the piece of medical equipment. The doctor looked down at his chest where the elephant lay. He glanced back up at Robert, his eyes twinkling.

"I'd forgotten I had old Bar-bar on today! Hello, I'm Doctor Bald-Eagle. You must be Robert. Christie mentioned his fiancé might be bringing Frankie in sometimes. I see that you're here for a sick visit. What seems to be wrong today?"

He would not swear in front of Frankie. He sucked in a

lungful of air to center himself.

"As I told the woman on the phone, repeatedly, this is a simple follow-up visit. Frankie fell yesterday while she was at the playground with the sitter. There was some glass and she got quite a gash on her forehead, right up at the hairline. Ally—that's the sitter—took her to the ER at E.J. Noble and they put nine stitches in. The home care instructions were very clear, but the daycare..."

The doc waved his hand at Robert. "They won't take her back or give her meds to her without a doctor's note and explicit instructions."

Robert blinked at the man. The doctor smiled sympathetically as he lifted Frankie out of Robert's arms.

"I have to apologize for not being better prepared when I came in to see you. We're running short on nursing staff today, and I told them I'd just get the info when I came in. I'm truly sorry it's made your first foray into follow up care from the ER more trying. And Christie must be deployed if you're bringing her in, yes? Don't worry, it gets easier."

Robert didn't know whether to be pleased that Christie had obviously felt certain enough of their relationship to let Frankie's doctors know he'd likely be in charge of her while Christie deployed, or irritated Christie had never mentioned this good looking doctor.

The doctor looked up after a moment from his perusal of Frankie's stitches. His friendly smile slipped a bit when he registered Robert's own unsmiling mien. A puzzled expression flitted across his face momentarily before clearing. He held his hand up. The gesture was both annoying and oddly soothing at the same time.

"Mr. Lindstrom, Robert—Doctor Maynard recommended Christie talk with me when he first...when Frankie's mothers died and he became a full time single parent. Something similar had happened to me, and it helped him to have a non-judgmental, non-military ear to bend when he was feeling overwhelmed. I really can't say more than that. Suffice it to say I am as much Christie's doctor as I am Frankie's."

He paused and tickled Frankie under her arm. She giggled delightedly. He set her gently back into Robert's arms.

"Dr. Maynard is on maternity leave, and as I'm the doctor in the practice most familiar with the Collins family, she asked me to take over their case for her until she returns."

Robert's face flushed. This day just kept getting better and better. He wasn't sure what his problem was. He was usually so much better with people.

"I'm sorry if I seemed rude Doctor—is that really your name?"

Shit. Robert slapped a hand over his mouth. Doctor Bald-Eagle's eyes widened minutely.

"I'm so sorry. I'm really not usually such an as—um, donkey… well, you know."

The doctor chuckled. The rich, deep sound eased Robert's tension somewhat. He waved off the apology. Reaching over, he gently patted Frankie's head, being sure to avoid the sore section.

"Don't worry about it. I've heard much worse in my day. I'll have a note for the daycare and some scripts instructing them on how to give the meds. Do you need something for your job as well?"

Robert nodded his head. He wouldn't have thought of that himself. It wasn't strictly necessary, but it would look better to have it in his file to explain his late call-in than just his say-so about the accident and the daycare.

"Thanks, Doctor Bald-Eagle."

The gorgeous doctor smiled wryly. "You're very welcome Mr. Lindstrom."

Picking up his laptop, he began typing information into it as he turned away. After a moment, he made his way briskly out of the room.

Robert sat for a moment, looking out the door in the direction the doctor had gone. His stomach ached. Every day he was faced with some new thing about Christie that he learned in the man's absence. Every time it happened he felt Christie's absence more keenly. How much work was it going to take to fit their little family together properly when Christie finally came home?

CHAPTER SEVENTEEN

The first thing Christie did as soon as the communications blackout was lifted was to write Robert a letter. The second thing he did was to rip it up. He wrote another one and let it sit on his desk for two days before he tore it up too. He wrote a letter every night that week, and then promptly tore them all up. Evans caught him at it on the eighth night when he came to see if Christie wanted to go do laundry with him. They'd both been avoiding the beer tent on the nights it was open, and discovered that when the beer tent was going, the laundry room was empty. Score.

Evans tapped on the heavy fabric of the curtain around Christie's bunk. When Christie grunted at him, he pulled it back. He gaped at all the shreds of paper on the floor, and shook his head.

"Fuck, Collins, you haven't written your guy yet? You gotta write him. Just…I dunno man, talk about the easy stuff."

Christie looked up at Evans and contemplated busting his lip. Evans saw the look and shrugged.

"Don't be an asshole, Collins. Write whatever, you know? He's gonna know the blackout's over, the family readiness group will be telling them back home what our APO address is. Just fucking write to him."

So Christie did.

His hands shook, and he threw up twice. Evans read the first line, and shook his head.

"What? Fuck, Evans; I don't know what to say. Hiya babe, I almost ended up burnt meat last week and then I almost fucked Evans, turns out Bergitta was right about me after all. I'm nothing but a heart-breaking whore?"

The next day Sergeant Tarans put them both on extra-duty for fighting.

It wasn't like they could deny it, both of them sporting shiners and split lips.

After they cleared up all the trash in front of their row of tents, Evans gave Christie some pointers on less likely to break his engagement type things he could say.

November 1ˢᵗ-on communication monitoring duty

Dear Robert,

I miss you. The communication blackout is over. Yeah, obviously right? Anyway, I …I know it sounds stupid, but would you send me a shirt of yours? One you worked out in? Shit. I sound like a freaking middle school girl. I'm not sleeping too good babe. I think maybe, if I could smell you and Frankie, like I was home in bed you know (?), it would help me sleep. Yeah, it's stupid, but please just do it. Hah! Like a Nike commercial, right?

Very Embarrassed, Christie

Robert laughed in delight at Christie's Nike joke. His letter was the best part of a completely craptastic day. Hal Byer's wife finally lost her fight with cancer and the man was a wreck. The captain actually had to relieve him of his weapon and order him to get counseling. Then he got a flat on the way home and when Ally sassed him he'd just…roared at her. Goddess help him, it even hurt to look at Frankie tonight.

November 21ˢᵗ

Christie,

*I miss you too baby. Anything you need lover. Honestly, it makes sense to me. I kept a shirt of yours out of the wash, and I've been sleeping with it ever since you left. *grin* Seriously, my sexy lover, I'd never think of you as either a middle schooler or a girl. Not with that beautiful man-sized cock you're packing. I sent you a shirt of Frankie's too. They're sealed up in plastic baggies. Nikki said that might make the smell last longer. I hope you don't mind I asked her. She's cool about stuff like that. I put a jock of mine* *in too, in case you need something to jack off with. (Don't worry; I didn't tell Nikki that part.) I've been doing it in the bathroom at work because I keep worrying that Frankie will walk in while I'm doing it if I do it in bed at home. How the hell did you ever manage? I bet you just locked the door...I don't dare, you know how I just pass out after, and I'm such a hard sleeper. Was she walking before you left?*

Anyway, stay safe baby. Just stay safe and make it home to us. Nothing else matters.

Love, Robert

P.S. Mom said to tell you we're gonna have another Turkey Day when you get home, cause then we'll really have something to be thankful for. Gran says hello and the baby-wipes are from her. She saw on the t.v. how the soldiers need them, so...Bergitta said to keep your pecker in your pants (LOL). You know how she is. The bracelet is from Ally-Cat. She braided it from a lock of her hair. She swears it'll keep you safe.

Don't forget to think about whether you want to do the hand-fasting ceremony with me. It would mean a lot to me.

Christie jolted awake at 0400, gagging, the taste of burnt meat so thick in his throat he barely made it to his trash bag to empty his stomach. Fuck. He was so damn sick of seeing Jenkins every night. Why the fuck couldn't he dream about Robert and Frankie? He thought he caught a whiff of patchouli, but...Caro still wasn't speaking.

He flipped on his little mag-light and pulled a couple of sheets of paper off the shelf one of the engineers had built for him as a thank you for all his help during the cleanup.

Fuck.

Not thinking about that.

Christ on a cracker, he had to wait an hour before the cooks would be down at the dfac. They'd gotten so used to him mooching coffee before chow hours they usually had it poured for him when he got there. Christie didn't know their names though. He deliberately avoided learning them. He knew too many names already.

His mag-light battery died. Christie put his hoodie and sweats on and sat on his bunk singing the song Aunt Cate had sung to him after his parents died softly to himself. He waited for 0500 to roll around and then went to get a caffeine fix and a place to write his letter. He did not think about Bergitta and how he'd let her down, or keeping his cock in his pants. He sat and stroked the thin blond bracelet around his left wrist.

December 4ᵗʰ

Christ on a cracker with jalapeños and cheese, babe. We gotta come up with some kinda system for when you're gonna send me sexy stuff. I opened that box up right in the platoon's command tent after mail call. Sweet Hell, the guys are never gonna let me live this one down. Simmons stole your jock and ran it up the flag pole down at HQ. Don't worry though. We fixed Simmons good. His girl sent him a pair of her panties. It turns out Evans is pretty handy with a needle, so we put some Velcro on the back of Simmons's p.t. (physical training) uniform and stuck her panties on when he wasn't looking.

I thought Sergeant Tarans was gonna stroke-out. I didn't know a man could turn that shade of purple and still live. Evans and I will be on extra-duty for the next week, so I won't be able to call as we'll miss phone hours. Sorry babe. I wish you coulda seen Simmons face when he realized what was on his back. It was worth the extra-duty.

Still cracking up, Christie

P.S. I think the mail service is smoothing out.

P.P.S. Frankie is walking?

P.P.P.S. The hand-fasting actually sounds cool. My Aunt Cate will be in heaven. LOL. You have no idea.

Robert went in to talk to Judge Wallace himself when he found out the man was hearing the case against the guy from the farmer's market. One of the sheriffs who had shown up to arrest him had gotten mixed up evidently, because they were charging the kid with aggravated assault.

Fuck.

Christie would blow a gasket.

Robert swore out a statement. On the way home he picked up another bottle of Maalox. He'd run out that morning.

December 12ᵗʰ

Dear Christie,

I'm sorry about the phone calls. I missed hearing your voice. I also wanted to ask you about the cake. The cake lady (Kirsten) said what you wanted won't work for a summer wedding. She could do it if you want to switch to an inside venue, but at the outdoor one the frosting you want will melt off at that time of the year. I put in a picture of the one she wants to substitute. If you want me to just decide I will. I just wanted to make sure you like what we have. The Army liaison is really pushy. I want to punch the bastard in the mouth about once a day. You'd think it was his f***ing wedding.

Oh, fuck it. That's not fair. I just hate having to talk to him about the wedding stuff before I even get to tell you. This sucks Christie, and not in a good way. Gotta run baby, or I'll be late for my shift. I put your presents from Frankie and I in the box…she picked out the paper herself. I know it won't get there in time for Christmas…I'm sorry. It's been…hectic around here. So, even though Sharon from the FRG (family readiness group) told me I had to mail it last month…well, I dropped the ball. Open mine by yourself. I'd hate for poor Simmons to get embarrassed again. Try to stay outta trouble baby, so we can talk to you on Christmas.

Love you so much it hurts, Robert

When the call came down for NBC—chemical specialists to report to the mailroom, Christie and Evans were standing outside the command tent trying to decide if they were gonna do laundry that night or not. Sergeant Tarans heard their voices, and that was that.

It was the story of Christie's life lately. Wrong place, right time.

Shit.

There was something leaking all over a stack of boxes. Another chemical team –the air force guys—beat them down there and had already started checking everything over.

At least when he was in his mopp suit he couldn't smell anything but himself.

January 15ᵗʰ

I didn't get your package in one piece Robert. The ######### got ###### last fall, so when there's ########### ########## they're real strict about how we handle them. So anyway, when I talked to you on Christmas they sounded like real nice gifts. I bet you knew I was just pretending that I had got them on time. Never have been able to fool you.

Anyway, the package got trashed. The mail guys are cool though…they managed to find most of your letter.

Give the baby a kiss for me. Is she even a baby anymore? I guess when they start walking you can call them toddlers, right? I hope you're getting more of my letters than I am of yours.

Miss you, Christie

P.S. You know how they say war is hell? Fuckers were low-balling it.

0400 again. He was so damn tired. There was no point trying to go back to sleep though. Hell, he didn't much feel like writing Robert even. How many times could he tell Robert it was hot? Or that the camel spiders really grossed him out? So all he had left was what had happened, and why he couldn't sleep, and he didn't want that stuff anywhere near Robert or Frankie. Easier not to write until he could think about something else. Christie wrapped his arms around himself, and rocked, and sang. It brought enough calm to last him till the dfac opened. Sometimes it almost sounded like Caro was singing, real soft in the distance.

CHAPTER EIGHTEEN

Robert's hands shook as he opened the letter. The writing on the envelope was so different from the last letter he'd gotten from Christie that at first he thought someone else had written it. That made his heart pound. Tad, the pushy Army public relations liaison had told him not to worry, that he'd be informed immediately if something bad happened to Christie.

Robert knew better. Christie usually wrote at least twice a month. Sometimes he wrote nearly every day, and just mailed the multipage letters every couple of weeks. The last one...well, it had scared Robert. So much of it had been blacked out it hadn't really made sense. Just something about him and Evans being on a cleanup detail it sounded like, and that he hadn't gotten the Christmas package after all. The lines weren't even straight, some lines crossing over the top of the lines below them, making it even harder to read. Christie had beautiful handwriting. Or at least he used to.

Something was wrong.

Dear Robert,

I'm sorry I was too much of a coward to say what I need to your face. I want—no, I have to tell you, because you deserve to hear it from me and not that asshole Simmons.

Listen babe...the day before I called the first time some bad shit went down. The mailroom got bombed the day before I called that first time.

I dream it almost every night. It was ugly...and Evans and me were right there, and Evans took Sergeant Richards down the hill to the medics... And then Sergeant Tarans was pissed because we went to help, me and Evans, so he volunteered us to help clean up the mess.

Evans and me, mostly me, were on detail all that week. Well, bagging up our friends—or what was left of them down there at what had been the mailroom. The other mail guys were real grateful our platoon volunteered, and managed to find most of your letter. I think this letter will get to you intact…Bryant said he knew a way to get it through. Plus they told us we could talk about the bombing on the phone now, so…I figure it's okay.

Anyway, that night I got drunk—I'm not making excuses here. I just want you to get the whole story. I was so lonely. We were talking at the beer tent—me and Evans—just talking about Jenkins from the mailroom and how his wife had just had a baby…and I felt so dead inside. The next thing I knew we were down in the dark motorpool in the cab of my truck and kissing.

I stopped him Robert. When he went for my pants, I stopped him and I told him I couldn't because of you.

I'm not sure I would have told you, because it didn't happen all the way, and I know how bad this is gonna hurt you.

Simmons found out from an MP 'friend' he made who saw us that night, and he swore he'd tell you as soon as he got home. He wanted to get even with Evans and me because his girl's dad had a buddy over here who found out about the thing with her underwear. I guess they're real religious and her father won't speak to her and her mom just cries and asks her to read stuff about how fallen women can redeem themselves.

He was the one that started the practical jokes, but he would do something spiteful, the fucker. He was gonna come to your job and try to humiliate you in front of the guys you work with. I gather he has pictures. The MPs were testing out some night vision photographic equipment and Evans and me got to star in the trials.

I am so sorry. I couldn't let him embarrass you like that Robert. Evans said to tell you he's sorry too. That if he'd known before he tried it how much I was crazy about you he'd have been a better friend and helped me not be lonely as a friend instead of trying to fuck me.

I should never have kissed someone else.

I'll be home April 25th. This should get there at least a week or two before. I wanted you to have time to figure how you feel. I'll understand if you need to go away for a bit. I sent Aunt Cate a note asking her to call you and see if you need a break. She'll call on the 28th or 29th of March. That way if you don't want to see me, you don't have to. I do hope you give me another chance, though.

   Christie

The letter slipped from Robert's nerveless fingers. Today was April 4th. Christie had the timing down. Robert would have time before he came home to sort...fuck. To feel something other than numb. Tonight, numb might be good. He'd take up his mother's offer to give him a weekend to himself. He got up to pack a bag for Frankie, making sure she was playing contentedly in her playpen before he left the room. He'd drop her off in the morning, and then...He wasn't sure he'd be able to sort this out by himself at all. He detoured into his bedroom to pick up the phone. Robert called the one person he knew wouldn't judge either him or Christie, and just might be able to help him get some perspective.

"Hello? Nikki...I know it's a school night...but do you think Ally could watch Frankie for a few hours while you and I talk? We can even stay here...I'll start a fire in the portable fire pit... you'd better stop by the liquor store and pick up some Bailey's for me and some Kahlua for you. This is gonna require special coffee...yeah, I'll put the good Kona coffee on right now. What? Oh, yeah, food for the kids would be great. Thanks sis."

Twenty-eight minutes later Nikki showed up, a Little Caesars Hot-N-Ready pepperoni balanced on one hand, a bag from the local liquor store dangling from her other. Ally grinned up at him from beside her, gleefully clutching two kid's meals from Mickey Dee's. As she passed him, she winked up at him.

"Since it's an emergency Uncle Nalle, I'm giving you the discounted rate...you just hafta pay mom back for the food."

That actually dredged a smile out of him. Her mother made a choking half laugh sort of sound. Clearing her throat, she waited until Ally turned to look at her. Then she raised an eyebrow, looked pointedly in the direction of Frankie's room and said two words.

"Scram kiddo!"

Ally, looking not the least bit affronted at her dismissal, gave her mother a snappy salute. She turned to Robert and threw her arms around him, squeezed him tightly once and let go. Without further explanation she hustled off to the kitchen. Then, fast-food meals in one hand, one of Frankie's healthy, ready to eat toddler meals in the other; she made her way back past Robert and Nikki towards Frankie's room.

Nikki walked into the kitchen and grabbed some paper plates from a cupboard. Setting them on top of the pizza box she reached into the next cupboard over and pulled out two mugs. Glancing around, she locked eyes with Robert where he was still standing in the living room, feeling lost. She gave an exasperated grunt.

"Nalle, snap out of it big brother. I only have two hands. I need you to get the coffee in these mugs. Better yet, pour the coffee into that carafe I gave you as a moving-in-with-your-lover present, and bring it and the mugs out to the patio. I hope you got the fire going…it's not freezing out, but it's not exactly let's-lounge-on-the-patio weather either."

Robert got the carafe filled and even made it out to the patio. He was relieved to note he had managed to light a fire in the portable pit.

Nikki pulled the bag from the liquor store out of his reach when he tried to get to it. She shook her head at him. Then she pointed to the pizza and paper plates.

"Food first, Nalle, and then I'll let you at the liquor. Otherwise you'll get drunk too fast and instead of explaining your emergency to me you'll just get pissed and cuss or get sad and cry."

CHAPTER NINETEEN

Surprisingly, Robert found he was hungry. Something about Nikki's hard-won, hard-headed practicality eased the tight feeling in his chest. She might not have any answers, and she might not even be able to point him toward anyone who did, but she'd listen.

"Thanks Nikolina."

Nikki looked over at him. Raising one eyebrow sardonically, she waved her slice of pizza at him and chewed a moment more before swallowing. She shrugged one shoulder dismissively as she spoke.

"Huh. Thank me later Nalle, after we see if I can help."

Robert smiled at her as he finished off his second slice. "You already have Nikki."

He picked up the carafe, poured a cup, and then glanced questioningly at his sister. When she nodded her head he filled the second cup three quarters of the way full, pushing it across to her as soon as he was done. She smirked at him and passed the bottle of Bailey's over. Robert grabbed the bottle with one hand and her hand with the other.

Releasing her hand, Robert opened the Bailey's and poured a healthy amount into his coffee. He took a fortifying swig of it, and then pulled the letter from his pocket. Robert's hand clenched over the paper, trembling as he handed it over to her. Nikki read it silently, her brows pulling into a fierce frown by the time she finished. Setting it down she picked up the Kahlua and poured a splash into her coffee. She took a sip, set the cup down, and caught Robert's eye.

"So, do you believe him?"

Robert blew out a harsh breath. He chewed on the corner of his upper lip as he weighed his words. Catching himself at it, he shook his head. It seemed he'd caught some of Christie's quirks.

"I do… Nikki, I know Evans. We've had him here for dinner. I—what the fuck was he thinking? He's supposed to be Christie's friend, and from everything Christie said, and everything he didn't say…that's the part that hurts the most. Goddess, the man promised me he'd take care of Christie until they got back and I could take over. I-I think I'll beat the hell out of Evans if I see him anytime soon. When they come back will you pick them up?"

Nikki narrowed her eyes at him.

"So, we're going with the 'Evans is evil' defense?"

That surprised a laugh out of Robert.

"Not evil…just… Shit Nikki, you know I can't…it hurts more to be angry at Christie."

Nikki nodded her head briskly, the precariously balanced bun in her hair sliding off to the left and drooping a little more. She growled, pulled the scrunchie out of her hair and started immediately twisting the whole mess back up onto her head. A little frown formed between her brows.

"Yeah. I can see that. I'll take off the day they come home. I can pick Christie up. Besides, if I lose my temper I can hit Evans, yeah?" Nikki grinned tightly at him, her eyes glittering like a predator's. She was definitely gonna punch Evans. Shit. "No one will take it seriously. They'll probably all think I'm some pissed off former girlfriend he met through Christie."

Robert considered trying to talk her out of it. Part of him really wanted someone to plant a fist in Evans's face. He knew it was unreasonable to hold Evans entirely culpable and Christie entirely innocent in the whole thing…but Christie said 'I stopped him.'…and to Robert that said Evans had pushed the issue, and Christie had been forced to protect himself from the one guy there who should have had his back with no questions asked. He shrugged and smiled wryly at her.

"Try not to get banned from base permanently. That's where the wedding is being held…and I want you to be my best woman Nikki."

Nikki squealed and leapt at him. It was a neat trick, considering she'd done it from a seated position. Robert had thankfully just set his cup down, so his hands were free to catch her.

"Brat. One of these times I'm gonna miss. You know that, don't you?"

Nikki laughed up at him, her messy blond locks already falling down her back again. He pulled her in tight, tucking her head into the crook of his neck. He squeezed her until she squeaked.

"I was so scared when I got the letter Nikki. I thought it was a Dear John letter, you know? I thought I was losing him. It hurt so bad...he thinks Bergitta is right about him. Dammit, he should have trusted in us enough to tell me these things to my face."

Nikki pulled back slightly.

"Robert, he's young, and not so good with the saying what he feels. I mean, the man has a freaking wall of post-it notes to tell his dead friend how he feels. And as far as him not being good enough? We both know Bergitta doesn't think anyone is good enough for a Lindstrom, and we both know why."

Nikki's mouth turned down, tears glistening in the corners of her eyes. She pressed her lips together, blinking them back. Robert wanted to say something to comfort her. "Nikki, I—"

She cut him off very effectively by putting her hand over his mouth.

"Shut up, Nalle. Bergitta was as much a victim as I was, and no one saw that. She needed counseling just as much if not more than I did back then, and she still needs it now. I'm fine. I got Ally out of the whole mess. Bergitta isn't fine. She can barely stand to be in a room with me or Ally."

Robert stared down at his baby sister; this astounding, amazing woman who'd grown from a girl who had a good portion of her childhood stolen away. He leaned down and very gently kissed her cheek.

"You amaze me Nikolina."

Nikki laughed at him and pushed out of his arms. Her own eyes were suspiciously moist looking. She pursed her lips and shook her finger at him.

"Don't you start with me, cry-baby-bear. Your job here is to get Mom and Dad to put their foot down with Bergitta and make her go to see someone. Tell them it's hurting Ally, because it is. You worry about that, and I'll pick up little Mr. Almost-a-cheater-pants from base when he flies in. Well, I'll pick him up right after I have a quick word with his friend."

Robert picked up his mug quickly to hide his smile behind. He enjoyed the thought of Evans having to walk around the Army post with a black eye. One that everyone would know a little, tiny, fragile looking girl gave him.

"Bloody minded Valkyrie."

Nikki gave him that tight, feral little smile again. His sisters really were a fearsome lot. Robert was often thankful his mother hadn't succeeded in having seven of them. He was certain the modern world couldn't have handled seven fierce Lindstrom women all in one generation. In ages past perhaps it would have be a good thing; seven handmaidens for Odin, choosing the worthy from among every battlefield's slain. Now-a-days, Odin left modern man to his own devices. There would be no controlling his handmaidens. He shuddered at the thought. Nikki noticed, and her grin got a little tighter, a little scarier.

"It's in the blood, brother dear. It's in the blood."

"You know we can't hang out when we get home right?"

Christie bit into the side of his cheek. His chest ached at Evans' wince.

"I mean, not until Robert's okay with it. Fuck, man, you know I'd rather have you there to watch my six, but I'm sorry. He's gotta come first."

Christie looked over at his friend. He knew Evans didn't have a lot of friends on post. His left of center demeanor put a lot of the other Joes off. It especially freaked out the ones who weren't comfortable around anyone who wasn't straight. The 'homo-avoidant' ones weren't as bad as the homophobic ones…they weren't out to beat you up for liking dick, or, as with Evans, liking dick some of the time…but they weren't clamoring to jump on the buddy band-wagon either.

"Yeah Collins, I know. I'll miss you. Nobody else gets my Ethan Day references. Well, I imagine Sgt. Tarans would get them…but it's not like I can pal around with him."

Evans shrugged his shoulders. His body language was relaxed, but when he looked up Christie saw the turmoil in his eyes. They looked almost wild.

"It's okay you know Evans. To like both. It doesn't change who you are."

Evans smiled at him, but the smile didn't reach his eyes. He nodded toward the rest of their platoon, most of them clustered at the rear of the transport. Only Sgt. Tarans and the Lt. had sat near them.

"It changes how everyone else sees me. Even you. Especially you. How can that not change who I am?"

Evans was right. That hit like a kick to the solar plexus. Christie didn't want things to change. Why did it have to be so damn difficult?

"I was gonna ask you to be my best man. I-I still want to, Evans. I just don't know…"

Christie trailed off. He'd really screwed things up. Evans nodded and swallowed hard. He closed his eyes as if he couldn't bear to look at Christie. Reaching over, Christie put his hand on Evans's arm. He hated the subtle flinch he received in return.

"I really am sorry Evans. I promise I'm still your friend. I just have to get things straight with Robert first."

Christie closed his eyes and leaned his head against the window of the plane. He drifted in a grey, sort of semi-awake state for a while, and then the nightmare started up again.

Christie walked into the mail-room. Robert's package was coming today. He knew it was. The sun outside had been so bright. It took a moment for his eyes to adjust, but he could smell a thick over-cooked meaty smell long before he could see what caused it. Christie gagged on the taste sticking to the lining of his throat. He called out to his friend as he entered.

"Hey, Jenkins, what's going on? Man, don't you guys know you're not allowed to cook in here? It's against regulations, man. You got my package? It's coming today. Caro told me it'd be here, so I came to collect it."

His eyes finished adapting to the dim interior of the building. Jenkins was standing with his back to the counter. Christie could see right into his head. The whole back was open, hair, scalp, and underlying skull blown away. At Christie's call he lurched around like a puppet. His glassy eyes stared at Christie from a mass of burnt flesh that had once been Jenkins' face. Christie was screaming, and no one could hear him through his mask. Jenkins' mouth moved, wet grunts trickling out as he gestured to a different counter. The other counter was built of twisted metal shards. Simmons stood behind it, grinning. He had a picture of Robert on the wall by his station. Extending the first two fingers of his right hand, he pointed them toward Robert's likeness and made gunshot noises.

Christie jolted awake glancing wildly around for Jenkins, Simmons, and Robert. Evans pulled back, gave Christie a searching look before settling his hand back on the armrest between them. Christie reached over and grabbed onto his friends arm. The firm flexing of muscle under his hand soothed him.

Evans placed his own hand over Christie's where it rested on his arm and squeezed.

"I see you too love birds are back at it." There was the voice that habitually turned Christie's gut into a boiling cauldron of acid. "Guess I'll have to get my camera and grab a few candid shots to share with your fiancé, huh Collins? Maybe at his job, so all the other cops can see what a piece of shit he's marrying. Bet it'll do wonders for his career."

One moment Christie was sitting with his hand on Evans's arm, the next he had Simmons down in the aisle-way between the seats, cutting off the man's airway with a chokehold. Christie could see Simmons turning blue, but couldn't bring himself to care. He didn't even realize anyone had noticed what was going on until Sergeant Tarans stood next to him.

"Beautiful example of how to perform a takedown in close quarters don't you think, Lieutenant? Let Simmons up before you hurt him permanently, Collins. I don't think he'll need another lesson in close quarters hand to hand combat any time soon, will you, Simmons?"

Christie released his hold.

Simmons scrambled back, coughing and gagging. "N-no Sergeant Tarans, I think I got it this time." Simmons' voice rasped like his throat was made of sandpaper. "There's no need for me to do it again."

Sergeant Tarans' eyes narrowed. His fists clenched tightly, turning the knuckles white.

"It takes a good soldier to learn the lesson the first time Simmons," he said, his voice soft. The sergeant's eerily calm tone made the hairs on Christie's head stand on end. "A decent one can learn it eventually, even if it takes longer than it should. I'd hate to start thinking you're not fit to be called a decent soldier."

Sergeant Tarans fell silent for a moment.

"Evans, take your battle buddy up to the front and get him a cool drink from the fridge those Air Force boys think we don't know they have on this air-bus." Sergeant Tarans kept his glare fixed on Simmons, his approval coming across only in his tone. "See if they have a half-way clean cloth you can wipe that blood off his face with too. It wouldn't do to land and have to parade Collins in front of the sergeant major of the post looking like that."

Evans popped out of his seat like a jack-in-a-box, pulling Christie up and hustling him toward the front of the plane past scraps of conversations floating up from the back of the transport.

"Scrappy little fucker…"

"…did you see…"

"Boom!"

"Simmons went down like…"

Then Evans had him through the curtain that closed off the front section of the transport's seating area. The flight staff that was there looked up at them curiously. Evans gestured at him.

"Our platoon sergeant told me to bring him up here and get him a cold drink and see if you had something I could clean him up with."

One of the men nodded and indicated they could sit in the empty seats up by him. He disappeared into the galley for a moment. When he returned he had two ice cold Cokes in his hands. He passed one to Evans and one to Christie. He also had a wet cloth in his hand which he passed to Evans along with a baggie full of ice.

"You might wanna put that on his eye…damn, what does the other guy look like?"

Evans just shook his head, pushed Christie down into a seat, and opened his can of soda for him. Christie still couldn't remember what had happened between Simmons snotty remark and Sergeant Tarans talking to him. That scared him worse. Evans started wiping blood off Christie's chin and the side of his face.

"The other guy is still alive. I think it's mostly because Collins here always listens to his platoon sergeant. I don't think he would have stopped for anyone else. I know he didn't hear me."

He finished wiping Christie's face and pressed the Coke Christie had distractedly set down back into his hand. Christie took a drink and looked up at Evans. It seemed a long way to where the other man sat on the arm of Christie's seat.

"You were too far away, Evans. Sergeant Tarans was the only one close enough for me to hear."

Evans gave him a worried look. That was okay. Christie was worried too. He was pretty sure if Sergeant Tarans hadn't noticed quickly enough he would have killed Simmons for threatening Robert, again. The worst part was he didn't think he would have felt one iota of remorse over it.

CHAPTER TWENTY

When Christie stepped out of the on-post air terminal, the first person he saw was Nikki. He looked past her for Robert's tall form and came up empty. Robert wasn't here. The smile stretching his lips fell away. As he drew closer, Nikki drew in a deep breath, hard and fast, her eyes roaming over his battered face.

"Christie, what happened to your face?"

Christie reached up and touched the split on his lip. He hadn't seen his face yet. It must look pretty bad, judging by Nikki's reaction.

"He was teaching that fucker Simmons to mind his own business." Evans smirked. "I mean he was teaching Simmons how to do a proper take down in a confined area."

Nikki's eyes narrowed, laser-like, on the name stitched onto his uniform. She smiled. There was something in that smile that Christie thought he should remember... only to register after it was too late. Bergitta had worn that expression when she'd first seen him, before he'd gotten to the root of her need to protect her siblings from outsiders.

Nikki had already stepped past him, already swept Evans's legs out from beneath him and popped him a good one in the eye on his way down.

Shit.

"Christ on a cracker, Nikki, what in the hell are you doing?"

She blinked at him insouciantly, and then nudged Evans's prone form with the toe of her boot. Her steel-toed black combat boot pushed into Evans's side a second time and Christie jumped to intercede. The capacity to be truly frightening was apparently a trait all the Lindstrom women shared.

"Nikki, please don't hurt him. He's my friend."

"Christie, your taste in friends has gone downhill since the last time I saw you. This piece of trash has caused a lot of trouble and strife…"

Evans groaned. Christie bit his lip and gave Nikki a pleading look as he reached a hand down to help the prostrate man back to his feet. His stomach churned, hot curls of acid stirred until they seethed like a pit of poisonous snakes.

It had all happened so fast. He hoped no one but him, Evans, and Nikki knew what had just gone down here. Shit. Some of the other soldiers were headed their way. Evans would be so embarrassed. Christie waved away the others that were headed toward their little group. Sergeant Tarans stood at the edge of the group, assessing the situation. He smiled weakly at the platoon sergeant.

"Then you better hit me too Nikki. I'm just as much…no, more to blame. He wasn't the one who had someone waiting at home."

"Nah, little sugar-bear, Robert said, well, he implied I could hit this one. He'd never let me hit you, no matter how much you fucked up. Besides, if I did it would just hurt him."

Evans finished clambering to his feet. He glared at Nikki for a moment. After a moment his angry gaze softened as he looked her over thoroughly. He breathed in deeply, nostrils flaring. He swayed slightly toward her, squaring his shoulders and firming his jaw.

"I guess you must be Robert's sister."

Nikki looked him over, a faint flush rising on her cheeks. Christie held his breath, hoping she would let Evans leave in one piece.

"Fine, Christie. I won't kick your so-called friend's ass. Bring your gear to the Jeep, Evans. We'll drop you at the barracks on our way off post."

Christie nearly choked on his shock.

Christie followed Nikki's lead to the car, sliding tentatively in.

He hadn't thought about Nikki knowing.

Oh shit.

Did Ally know? Bergitta?

Nikki looked over at Christie where he sat in the passenger seat. She smiled at him, easy, like it had always been between them. It was the first expression of hers he'd really been able to judge since laying eyes on her today.

"I'll drop you off at your place afterwards, little sugar-bear. Robert's waiting for you. He just got your letter a few weeks ago. He hasn't had time to completely sort out his feelings yet. Give him a little more time, okay? Mostly he's just scared. It would kill him to lose you…especially like that."

Christie closed his eyes. He couldn't bear to look at either of them right now. Nikki looked too much like her brother, and Evans looked like the sum of all his sins. He leaned his head against the window and pretended to sleep.

Robert heard Nikki's noisy old Jeep pull up in front of the house. He stayed on the patio, smoking his fourth cigarette of the day. He'd really thought when he quit the last time that he wouldn't start again, no matter what, but this concurrence of events was far outside of what he'd planned for. Darkness had fallen since Nikki left to pick Christie up. Though the flight had originally been expected in early in the morning, Nikki had been sent home around ten a.m. There had been some sort of delay which held them up in Spain. A phone call had come around noon telling Robert that the new expected time of arrival was five-forty-five p.m. Two hours later at nearly eight p.m., Frankie was already asleep. Christie's keys sounded in the lock. Robert braced himself.

"Robert? Where are you?"

Robert took another drag on his cigarette. Christie must have seen the glow of the ember. He dropped his duffle in the entryway of the kitchen and walked over to the patio doors. He didn't say anything about the cigarette; just bit his top lip worriedly. Robert watched the agitation on his face from where he sat, half turned toward the sliding glass door.

"I just need to see Frankie…she's in bed I suppose?"

Robert nodded. He didn't have it in him to answer with words yet. He was scared he'd start yelling. Christie continued to look at him for a moment longer, his blue-green eyes huge in his face. Then he turned away and started to walk into the living room again.

"I just got her down. Please don't wake her." Robert took a perverse sort of pleasure at the tension radiating through Christie's shoulders. "She hasn't been sleeping well the past few nights."

He could've told himself he didn't want to want Christie to be tense. Robert refused to lie to himself though. He liked that his lover was uneasy. That chicken-shit letter had made him feel tense. It was unacceptable for Christie to say the only reason he was telling Robert about the whole ugly incident was because someone else forced his hand.

Robert took another drag, trying to unclench his jaw. Christie watched him with narrow eyes.

"I think I know how to deal with my daughter, Robert." That razor edged comment sent a painful sensation, white-hot and jagged, lancing through Robert's chest.

"Funny, since I thought we were planning a life together, I thought she was our daughter now, Christie."

Christie flinched as if struck, his fists balling. Robert hated the way that hollow pain seemed to echo in his own belly.

Robert held his hands up, unsure if Christie could see them. He wished he could snatch the words back, unsay them. There was no way to do that though, and no way to undo what was done.

"I'm sorry Christie." He spoke quickly. They needed to find a way forward from here, not tear each other to shreds. "Go see

Frankie. She really hasn't been sleeping well the past couple of nights…I think she was picking up on how worried I've been about you."

Robert ground out the cigarette. What good would poisoning his body do?

"I'm so damn glad you made it home safe. Just—just go see her. Then we can talk if you're not too tired."

Christie disappeared into the house. Robert sat and waited, as he'd been doing ever since Christie had left over six months prior. He had no idea how to move forward from where they were if Christie couldn't start trusting him enough to tell him what was actually going on behind those beautiful blue-green eyes.

Christie stood just inside the door to Frankie's room. Robert had turned it into a wonderland for any child. Before the room had only held the crib, a changing table, and a small dresser. Now there was a little reading nook in one corner with big floor pillows propped in one corner, white mesh nets full of colorful stuffed animals hanging in every corner, and Frankie's crib had been converted into a toddler bed. Christie was astounded to see there was even a mural wrapped around the walls and fanned out across the ceiling.

Robert was here, doing all this for Frankie while Christie couldn't be, and he repaid him with that awful crack about her being Christie's daughter. He was such an ass. Christie hoped Robert could forgive him…for everything.

He stood there for a few more moments, gathering his courage. Once he scraped a little bravery up, he made his way back through the house toward the patio. Robert was still sitting in the same spot. The smell of smoke still lingered in the air.

Robert didn't smoke.

"Well, he had quit…looks like this thing with you is driving him to pick up bad habits again. He probably would rather smoke than choke the shit out of you."

You're probably right Caro. I-It's nice to ummm…see you again.

"Dork. You can't see me. I know what you mean though. Don't think this means I'm done being pissed at you."

I'm okay with that Caro. Just don't—don't leave me again. I really missed you.

"Christie, I have a news flash for you. You went a little nutty over there, and I couldn't stand to be around you for a while."

Well, you still shouldn't have left me on my own, Heifer. You know I don't do well on my own.

"No Christie, you really don't."

Christie slid open both the glass and screen doors to the patio and stepped out to face Robert, and the mess he had made of their relationship. He walked over to sit on the stool next to Robert's. It surprised him to be stopped with an arm around his waist.

"Sit with me Christie."

Christie bit his lip. A flare of hope lit up inside him. It had to be good that Robert wanted to hold him while they talked. Sitting down, Christie spent a moment absorbing the feel of Robert surrounding him again after so long. Christ, he'd missed the heat of Robert's big body soaking into him.

"I'm sorry Robert."

CHAPTER TWENTY-ONE

Robert bit the inside of his cheek. He wanted to just tell Christie it was okay, that everything would be fine, but he wouldn't start lying to the man now. It wasn't all fine.

"I know you're sorry, baby. It still hurt me badly. I think the worst part is that you wouldn't even face me to tell me. Why did you send me a letter saying you wouldn't have told me if you thought you could get away with it? Do I mean so little to you?"

Christie seemed to try to burrow right into him for a moment. Then he slid his arms around Robert's waist, anchoring himself there and leaned back to look into the taller man's face.

"I was scared that I wouldn't tell you Robert. Terrified that Simmons would manage to surprise you with the news about what had happened because I'd been too fucking dumb to simply man up and tell you what went down with Evans. If he had gotten to you, made it seem like Evans and I were together, like I wanted to leave you…I'd have killed him. And I knew if you found out from someone else that I would lose you for sure. I—I haven't got any pride left where you're concerned. I don't even have want left for you…only need."

Robert reared back as if he'd been struck. Christie didn't want him. His eyes stung and his throat seemed scraped raw. The inside of his mouth tasted hot and coppery. It was the metallic sweetness of blood. Robert had bitten right through the soft flesh of his inner cheek. His arms reflexively closed tighter around Christie, and then he forced himself to relax his hold, allowing the younger man to get away whenever he wanted to.

"I understand Christie."

"No you don't, Robert. You think I…I don't know what you're thinking, but if it makes you look like you are right now, whatever it is, you're wrong."

Robert spent a moment chasing that convoluted logic.

Wait. What?

Christie's arms around his waist tightened again, pinching slightly. Robert opened eyes he'd closed without realizing. He looked down at Christie, and saw the frown marring his beautiful face.

"I really don't think you do understand Robert. When I left back in October I knew that I loved you. I didn't know that I couldn't breathe without you. That sounds stupid…but my lungs don't …shit, I sound like a middle school girl again."

Robert laughed. He couldn't help himself. His lover was so damned absurd. Only Christie would be making grand statements about how he only breathed because of his love and in the middle of it all ramble off about feeling like a pubescent girl. He leaned down to kiss the tip of Christie's nose. Christie tilted his face up, quickly changing Robert's gentle reassurance.

Christie opened his mouth on a needy moan, and Robert was helpless to stop himself from slipping his tongue inside. His arms seemed entirely disconnected from his conscious mind at this point. They scooped Christie's lithe body tight against his, wrapping tight as steel bands around lean shoulders and waist. Robert fell into the kiss with abandon. He could wait to find out exactly what Christie meant. For now it was enough to know that what his lover felt ran so deep he classified it as need. He found both his hands on Christie's firm ass, kneading the resilient flesh as equally hungry groans poured from his throat.

The small, fearful knot in Christie's chest melted for the first time in months in the face of Robert's passionate heat. They had a lot to work out. There was no way it was going to be all sunshine and roses all the way to their very public wedding, but maybe they were back on the path that would lead them there. Christie pulled his mouth away from Robert's for a moment.

"I need you now. I-we have so much to talk about but I can't wait. Now, Robert. I need you right now."

Robert nodded and stood with Christie in his arms. He paused at the sliders long enough for Christie to lean down enough to pull them open, and then stepped through. He didn't stop once inside and the doors stood open behind them. Christie couldn't bring himself to care. Robert walked straight to the bedroom. Christie expected to be launched through the air and bounce on the bed a few times before Robert's weight came down and settled him against the mattress. He was shocked when Robert managed to exhibit enough restraint to set him carefully onto the comforter.

His lover's normally cerulean eyes had darkened to a color nearer navy. How his big Norse godling managed to treat him so tenderly while so obviously aroused was beyond Christie. The calm at his center caught fire at the sight of Robert stripping off his clothes while watching Christie with smoldering eyes.

"Every night you were gone I'd lay in that bed and think of you while I touched myself. Do you know what I want Christie? I want to watch you do the things I did to myself while I lay there thinking of you."

Christie swallowed. Holy fucking Christ. He was burning alive, and Robert just kept turning the flames higher and higher.

"After I put the baby to bed Christie, I'd come in here and fall back on the bed. I'd lay there a while thinking of the last time we talked. Close your eyes Christie, like I did."

Robert's voice was a low rumble of desire that was inexorable, inevitable. "Run your hand up from your hip. Go slow across your stomach. Rub your nipples lightly through the thin cotton of your shirt. They'll start to stand up—that's when I want you to reach for the first button."

Christie was panting already. His cock pressed against the placket of his cargo pants so hard he was sure he'd have an imprint of all four buttons on the underside of his shaft. He traced his hands along the exact path Robert described. It got hard to focus, but thankfully he came to the last button while he still had some control over his fine motor skills.

"Once I had my uniform shirt unbuttoned, I'd push my

undershirt up with one hand until I could pinch my nipples. Do it Christie."

Christie gave a needy gasp. He did as Robert asked, hoping his lover would let him unbutton his cargo pants before he came in them. A patch of wetness was already spreading from the leaking head of his cock. He looked up at Robert in the most beseeching manner he could muster.

Robert smiled at him. He had his own shirt completely off at this point and his pants unzipped. Pulling his stiffening length out of his boxer briefs, he began a slow stroking motion up and down the shaft. Christie whimpered.

"Then, I'd reach one hand to the front of my pants. I'd open them up baby, just as fast as I could, 'cause by this point I'd be needing bad. I'd pull my dick out and squeeze it at the base."

Christie hung on his every word. He was panting loudly at this point. He started to stroke himself.

Robert nodded. He stroked himself a little faster. He licked his lips at the same time as Christie, his expression dark with hunger.

"Yeah, baby, that's right. Stroke it just like that. I would close my eyes and pretend you were here, begging to suck me off."

Christie broke at that. Scrambling to his hands and knees, he crawled to the end of the bed and tumbled off. Landing in an untidy heap at Robert's feet did not slow him down. He rolled, pushed himself up, and shucked Robert's pants the rest of the way down along with his boxer briefs.

"Please Robert…I need to taste you. Let me taste you?"

Robert placed a hand at the back of Christie's trembling head. He pressed against the back, urging Christie forward.

"I wouldn't make you beg for long. After you begged pretty for me one time like that, I'd nod and let you swallow me down…"

Christie suited his actions to Robert's words. He loved the taste of Robert's pre-come. He had forgotten how it tasted sweet and musky all at once, how perfect it was. He swirled his tongue around the head, pausing to lap at the delicious fluid seeping from the tip. He'd thought he'd never taste it again.

"I...I hold your head still..."

Christie rolled his eyes up to see Robert's expression. The hectic red staining his cheeks, flared nostrils, and dilated pupils spoke eloquently of arousal.

"...and you let me know it's okay, by nodding..."

Christie bobbed his head, swallowing Robert's cock to the root. Then he bared his teeth, raking them gently up the length of Robert's cock. Robert's moan turned Christie's blood to molten lava.

"...that I can fuck your mouth any way I want..."

Christie moaned around Robert's cock. Robert's control finally snapped. His big hands locked onto either side of Christie's head and he began to move in earnest. That hard grasp triggered the muscles of Christie's lower jaw and throat to release every bit of excess tension. As Robert began snapping his hips back and forth fucking Christie's face almost brutally, the smaller man moaned again. He was burning to fill his mouth with Robert's taste. Moisture welled in Christie's eyes. His heart was too damn full to hold it all in.

"Aaah...and...you love it...you beg with your eyes...and... unnh...as I start to—to come...you reach behind yourself, you—"

Christie was pretty sure he knew what Robert wanted. He pushed two fingers into his mouth, wetting them alongside Robert's cock. Once he had them slicked up, he reached behind himself to shove them into his own ass. The delicious burn as they went in forced another moan from him. The big trooper shoved his cock fully into Christie's mouth, pressing past his soft palate and into his fully relaxed throat as he began to shoot stream after stream of come. Christie swallowed, massaging the head of Robert's pulsating shaft, then pulled back to savor the intoxicating, salty flavor. Christ, this stuff packed a punch stronger than any drink he'd ever had. Christie dangled right on the edge of satisfaction. Then he pumped his fingers twice more into his ass, and he was coming as well, screaming around Robert's cock.

CHAPTER TWENTY-TWO

Robert's knees nearly gave out on him. He locked them, shudders still racking his body from the intense orgasm Christie had just brought him to. Holy Goddess, his sweet baby had a talented mouth. The reality of Christie being here with him was so far beyond any fantasy he could ever come up with. He wouldn't care if Christie traded his sweetly fuckable mouth and glorious blue-green eyes for something entirely different...except as it would affect Christie.

"Christ on a cracker, Robert. You melted me."

Christie had slumped down onto the floor. Robert kept his smile on the inside this time. He squatted down, scooped Christie up, and stood. He held Christie tight to his chest with one arm, using the other hand to pull the comforter back. Robert tucked Christie under the covers and slid in beside him, pulling the smaller man flush against his side.

"I get that you're sorry Christie. But what, exactly, are you sorry for? Are you sorry that you were tempted? Or are you sorry that you wanted to lie to me about what happened? I'll tell you right now that neither of those is as important as the fact you were frightened to face me. That's the one that really worries me, baby. The first one is nothing. Everybody gets tempted. I was tempted while you were gone. It was easier for me to deny it. I had some powerful incentive. I was surrounded with mementos of our life together. I was actually at the pediatrician's office, holding Frankie in my lap at the time."

Christie boggled at him. He opened and closed his mouth a few times. He didn't seem to know if he wanted to be angry or astonished.

"Doctor Bald-Eagle? You had the hots for Doc Bald-Eagle? Christ on a cracker Robert, he's my freaking therapist!"

Robert would have been worried by the words if Christie hadn't been chortling as he said them. He was glad Christie wasn't too freaked out by who he'd been tempted by, but he still needed to keep the younger man paying attention to the real issues here.

"Focus on the important stuff here Christie. The point is I was tempted too. The temptation is a non-issue for me baby. Can you let go of it?"

He liked that Christie didn't give him an automatic answer. It was crucial that he take his time and give answers that meant something real. Ones he had put a fair amount of thought into. After weighing the question Christie nodded.

"I think I can Robert. I'm willing to try if you really feel that way."

Robert paused to kiss Christie before he responded. Christie's voice had sounded shaky, just a little. It was as though he was having trouble believing it could be so simple.

"I really do feel that way. More important to me is that you would have lied to me if you thought you could have gotten away with it. That bothers me even more than the thought of you making out with Evans."

Christie grimaced.

"I…shit, Robert, I've known since it happened that it was just fucking stupid. I'm sorry. And Evans and I…Nalle, we fixed things between us. He's my best friend after you. And I want him to be my best man if it won't ruin the whole thing for you. He—I don't know what I would have done without him. I just…"

Robert bit back his first answer which was *fuck no he can't be in my wedding, not after he betrayed your friendship…and mine…* and tried to weigh how he felt against how Christie felt. He hated the idea of allowing a man who'd attempted to steal his future husband from him to play such an important part in his marriage. He thought he might have a solution if Christie was willing to go through the nonsense of doing it all twice in a relatively short span of time.

"I don't want him in my wedding, Christie. It's not just my wedding though. If we could have a hand-fasting celebration first though, or jump the broom at least, without him there, it would make me happy. If we could do that before the big mess the Army PR folks have set up for us, it would be perfect. If we can do one or both of those things, I can deal with having him be in the traditional mainstream wedding."

Christie looked confused. He was frowning again and wrinkling the bridge of his nose in the adorable way that Robert loved so much. It was so cute and sexy it made Robert want to forget the conversation and just get back to the sex. He knew they needed to work through this stuff though, and that started with talking through it at least once. Christie's expression cleared up after a moment.

"We talked about this one night didn't we? You want us to jump over a broom to sweep away the past, right? I don't remember some of the stuff that happened while I was over there."

Robert was confused now. Christie had written him about this conversation. How did he not remember it now?

"Robert, I know you don't want the whole big hoopla wedding. I really was going to try to keep it kind of small. For you. I—just can't now though, not with my command involved. I can do a little thing for you before…"

Christie's voice trailed off, and the tight skin around his eyes said he was holding something back. Robert didn't want that bit of tension to be about Evans coming to the handfasting. He let it drop. If it was important enough to Christie, he'd bring it back up.

Robert really thought this would be a sticking point for Christie. "Yeah baby…pretty much just like that. I…I didn't know you realized how I felt about the fancy cakes and tuxes. I want to do it for you though…because you wiggle when we talk about tuxes and fancy cakes, and I love to watch you wiggle."

Christie grinned at him, the tension easing from around his eyes. It was sweet and hot and so Christie it seemed unreal after so long without him. Robert grinned back, doing the mental math to figure out just how soon it would be kosher to start trying to get into Christie's pants again...not that he had any on. Heh. Good planning that. Robert was starting to get hard again. He shook off his lustful thoughts of Christie bound in the sling again, and tried to focus on the issues they needed to resolve.

"There is one thing that we didn't get to talking about though. I can't help but think that it's unintentionally deliberate. Why were you scared to face me baby?"

Christie looked at him like he was stupid. Robert loathed it when Christie gave him that look.

"Robert, I already told you why. I was scared I'd lose you, but I was more scared I'd chicken out and not tell you. That Simmons would hurt you more than just finding out would. So I wrote to stop Simmons and make it so I couldn't chicken out."

He might not have said it, but Robert could hear the 'well, duh' rolling in the air between them. Yeah, he'd been an idiot. Christie had been saying that all along. Still...

"It hurt Christie. Don't do that to me ever again, you hear me?"

Christie curled into him, spreading kisses along his throat and up to his chin. He didn't realize until the tension started to leave how tightly he'd been holding his jaw. He'd had his jaw clenched to the point it had started to give him a headache.

"I won't Robert. Not ever again."

Robert let the delight bubble up inside him. He was getting his Wiccan wedding, and they were going to do it first, so the mainstream wedding would just be another ridiculous work function he went to in support of his husband's career. He could do that and not even feel resentment. Trying to keep the 'na-na-na, I win' smile inside didn't work for him however. He finally just let it out.

"Well, then I guess we can start working on the big dumb thing for your job. I can take care of the Wiccan celebration by calling mom. She's an ordained priestess, so she can do the ceremony unless you object."

Christie just nodded his acceptance of that scenario and let his lips curve up in a small secret smile. Robert wondered if he'd drifted off as he did sometimes. He hadn't even reacted to the bold proclamation that they would be having a pagan ceremony as their actual wedding.

CHAPTER TWENTY-THREE

"He wants to kiss you, he's past wanting to date you, he wants it forever, wants a life-long mate oooh, he's the one who will hold you and cherish, all your quirks and all your foibles, he puts up with your tantrums and all of the trouble..."

Caro's little sing-song rhyme was bouncing around in Christie's head as he watched the play of emotions on Robert's face. He could hear his beautiful Nordic lover talking, but Christie wasn't paying any attention to the words. He just nodded and smiled at what he thought were the appropriate moments. All he could think of was how much he wanted to lick every inch of Robert's skin, only stopping when the big man pressed him down to the bed and fucked him silly.

He could so get behind that. Or better yet, he could get under that, or in front of it, or bounce around on top of it...

"Christie, are you day-dreaming again? I swear it's a good thing I'm a pretty self-confident guy or you would shred me."

Christie blinked at Robert. Damn Evans and his habit of listening to that funky, jazz inspired rap of William Shatner's. Christ on a cracker, how was he supposed to explain this drift to Robert? He knew better than to let Evans's name out of his mouth right now.

"Uh...I'm sorry Robert. I was thinking about William Shatner. You know, his song, _I can't get behind that!_ ...well, I was thinking I could get behind you getting behind me right about now."

Christie's face was burning hot and probably cherry red. He wasn't sure about the color, because there wasn't a mirror in his line of sight. It was worth it though, because Robert's eyes were darkening to his _gonna fuck you now_ dark blue again. It was Christie's favorite color in the whole wide world.

"Christie, you didn't hear a word I said just now, did you?"

Christie hesitated. He figured the truth was his best option, even if it didn't get him what he wanted immediately.

Shit.

"No, Robert, I haven't a fucking clue what you said. I was too busy watching your mouth move and imagining you kissing me while you shoved that big, hard coc-"

His words got cut off. Robert twisted over the top of him, pressing their mouths together. The feeling of the bigger man's weight pressing him into the mattress was everything Christie had been aching for ever since he'd left for the deployment. A warm, wet sensation against his lips let him know Robert wanted in his mouth.

He heard a little snippet of the song in his head.

Christie snickered. He couldn't help it. Robert lifted his head up to glare down at Christie, who was still giggling.

"If I'm making you laugh, I'm not doing something right. If I'm doing it right and you still have the presence of mind to be laughing about something else, I need to up the intensity..."

Robert dove back into the kiss without bothering to finish his sentence. He burned hot enough against Christie it was like being branded. He dimly heard a snicking sound as Robert's tongue mapped the interior of his mouth. The warm thrust and retreat in his mouth had him so preoccupied he was startled when he realized it wasn't the only rocking motion he felt.

Robert lifted his head again. Christie whimpered in needy frustration. Robert had one slick finger sliding slowly in and out of him, pausing to circle the rim of his sphincter and then thrusting firmly back in. The finger in his ass felt good, but he wanted more. He was hollow inside.

"Please Robert. More. Need you to fill me everywhere."

Robert grunted, just fucking grunted and pulled his fingers out of Christie's ass. Christie didn't remember there being more than one in there, but evidently he'd lost a moment or two while his blond godling was stroking his prostate. Christie hissed in pain when Robert gripped his thighs to spread his legs apart.

There was a huge purple bruise on the back of the right side where Robert wouldn't have seen it. Not with him lying down. Christie figured he'd done something to it while he was taking Simmons down in the airplane.

"Where did you get that?"

Robert's voice was cautious. It was evenly pitched and studiously non-judgmental. Christie hated it. Every careful syllable marked a place where he had wounded Robert. He could explain a lot of coincidental shit if it helped Robert get past the one thing he could never fully explain, since he didn't fully understand it himself.

"I kind of lost it on the plane. I...um, Simmons was starting shit again and he said he was gonna bother you. One minute I was sitting down and then the next thing I knew I had him down on the floor in the aisle. I had him locked up in a choke-hold and I was just watching him turn blue, Robert. I wasn't thinking anything at all. I was just watching the color change in his face. I—I guess it must have happened then. In the time in-between, you know? I don't remember it."

Robert froze. The skin of his face seemed to pull tighter across his cheeks. The corners of his mouth pinched together. A shudder rippled across him, almost a flinch. Then he dove back down, tongue and cock both spearing into Christie at the same time. Christie cried out, overwhelmed at the fiery intermingling of pain and pleasure. It burned so good. He was beyond full, and Robert kept pushing more of himself inside, until it was like the bigger man would slide completely under Christie's skin.

Christie was so far past words all he could do was howl incoherently like some wild thing. He gave up, just flung his hands up above his head and relinquished all control to Robert.

His surrender seemed to immolate Robert. The older man burned with intensity, his normal control eradicated. His big hands flexed on Christie's thighs, biting into them as he pounded wildly into his smaller lover. The force of his thrusts moved Christie up the bed until Robert released his legs, letting them fall around the larger man's waist. Robert wrapped his arms under

Christie's, reaching up his back to grasp his shoulders. He pulled Christie into each thrust then with a jarring force just on the pleasurable side of too much.

Robert bit the side of Christie's neck hard, barely stopping before he broke the skin. Christie arched into it, loving the feeling of being possessed by Robert.

It was a damn good thing the bed was so sturdy.

Robert pulled him into a final thrust and then held him there as he roared and shook and ground his hips against Christie as he marked his lover from the inside.

The hot jets of Robert's essence set Christie's own climax off. He wailed out Robert's name repeatedly until he ran out of breath. He continued to shiver and twitch for several minutes afterward. Christie didn't think he could have explained it in any way that made sense to anyone but himself, but it made him feel clean, and safe somehow, to have Robert's sweat coating every inch of his body and the big man's come seeping out of him. It made him feel owned, and like he was snuggled up in the warmest, most tightly wrapped blanket in all of existence while a blizzard raged outside.

By the time Christie could have forced his shaking limbs to move, Robert had collapsed into a very heavy, gently snoring blanket. He wouldn't have attempted moving until morning if he hadn't heard Miss Kitty meowing outside the door. He listened to her plaintive mews for another couple of minutes while he wiggled his way out from under Robert. He grabbed Robert's robe, shrugged into it, and stumbled out to the kitchen to feed her.

Fancy Feast. Miss Kitty had moved up in the world.

Christie's lips curled up at this further evidence of Robert's being primo husband material. He knew as he settled back in he'd find more things like this. Robert had been doing things like this since their first date. Christie left the under the cabinet lights on so that Miss Kitty could see what she was eating and made his way back to his warm bed, where Robert lay sleeping. He slipped out of the ratty old robe Robert insisted was more comfortable than the plush new one his sister Bergitta had bought him. Then he wiggled his way back underneath Robert until the big man's weight was once again pressing him into the mattress. He fell asleep with more ease than he had in a long time.

Robert jolted awake, immediately caught up in fighting to hold a screaming, thrashing Christie down. It was long minutes before his Christie was looking at him again through those beautiful blue-green eyes. When he was sure Christie knew where he was, and who Robert was, he eased his hold on the smaller man. He had never been more grateful for the disparity in their size as he was right then.

Shit. If Christie had been even an iota bigger or stronger, Robert didn't think he could have held him long enough for the smaller man to realize where he was before something very bad went down. His upper lip stung where Christie had gotten a solid crack in before Robert woke up enough to hold him down.

Holy Goddess, the things Christie had been screaming.

"Christie, baby, are you okay?"

Christie pulled his head back, his eyes glazing over again for a second. Then he sort of quivered all over, a light sheen of sweat breaking out on his brow and above his upper lip. Finally, his eyes cleared. Blinking up at Robert, he struggled lightly against the bigger man's light hold.

"Robert, I know you like to get a little rough and kinky sometimes, but now probably isn't the best time. I'm still pretty sore from the thing with Simmons and Frankie will be up any minute now."

Shit. He acted as if he hadn't heard Robert's earlier question. Robert had seen troopers get like this once or twice after they'd gone through something really hairy. The worst one had been Ryan Lewinski after the hostage situation three years ago. Ryan had traded himself for, he thought, all the hostages. However, the bank robbers had kept three back to amuse themselves. They made Ryan watch what they did to them. He'd ended up leaving the troopers.

Christie was talking.

"...so, anyway, that's why I was so adamant about seeing her last night...I know all about the stitches, Robert. There was nothing Ally could have done to stop Frankie from falling on that glass."

Christie blinked.

"What happened to your lip?"

Robert gaped at Christie. He touched a finger to the stinging place on his lip. When he pulled the digit away, it was smeared with red. Great.

"Did the hospital notify your chain of command?"

Christie shook his head no.

"Christie, how did you find out? I meant to tell you... I got worried about how you were holding up over there."

"It's okay Robert. I get why you did it. That was why I had to see her when I first got home. I knew she was okay, I just didn't know she was okay, not in my gut."

Robert nodded. He got that. It still didn't answer one pertinent question.

"How did you know about it if the hospital didn't tell you? The hair's grown back where they shaved it to put the stitches in, and I know Nikki wouldn't have told you without checking to make sure I talked to you about it first."

Christie looked uncomfortable. "Promise not to have me locked up first."

Robert snorted. Christie rolled his hand, prompting a response.

"Okay Christie, I promise to hear you out. Even if I do think you've slipped a few gears, we'll just get a private shrink on my health insurance. Your chain of command will never have to know."

Christie rubbed Robert's arm, seeming to soothe himself as well as Robert.

"Caro told me."

CHAPTER TWENTY-FOUR

Robert wanted to laugh. He wanted this to be Christie having a dream that actually came true. Christie's freaky text-book accurate enactment of Post Traumatic Stress Disorder made him wonder. So did Christie's solemn eyes.

Shit. Did Christie think Caro was still alive? "Caro told you? Did you see her?"

His tone had to be off. Christie was starting to scowl.

His eyes went blank. The frown left his face, and he shoved Robert's shoulders, hard.

"You said you wouldn't judge."

Christie pushed away, fury tight in his frame as he stood.

"Dick. Lots of people see ghosts. That doesn't make me crazy."

Okay, his tone had been a little 'calm the crazy person down'. Robert held his hands up in surrender.

"Christie, baby, stop. I just misunderstood. Seeing ghosts isn't crazy. I didn't know you were a medium."

Christie froze in the act of scrambling into his pants. Robert blew out a relieved breath. He'd worried his volatile lover would be too angry to hear what he was saying.

Christie shot him a look that was this side of pure poison.

"I never said I was psychic. I don't hear other ghosts. I don't read palms or play with crystals and tarot decks. Caro...she says it's a fluke. That she stuck around to take care of Frankie and me."

These were the times Robert wondered if Christie only ever watched his lips move.

Robert shook his head at his young lover as he stood up from the bed "Did it ever occur to you that maybe I am into all that? I know I've told you about this…and you've met my family Christie… You really weren't listening last night when I told you why I wanted a handfasting, were you? I thought you were being a smart-ass…"

Robert's voice trailed off, his shoulders slumped and he sat back down on the bed with a thump.

Christie watched Robert in stunned silence. He had never seen the big man look so crushed, so…hopeless. Had he done that with his self absorption? Yes, there had been odd things at the Lindstrom's, and he couldn't help but know what they were as they looked similar to stuff his Aunt Cate had knocking around the house during the two and a half years he'd lived with her. But…he tried not to notice those sorts of things when he lived with Cate. Apparently, he'd gotten so into the habit that he'd ignored a big part of who Robert was.

Well, shit—he'd already told Robert he didn't remember a lot of stuff from the deployment. Maybe Robert would tell him those things again? He could write them down this time.

"Robert, I wasn't being smart-assed. I told you I wasn't paying attention…"

Robert held up a hand like a stop sign. Christie ignored it, sliding onto the bed and then right onto Robert's lap. He held his words in check however. That way he was at least honoring part of what Robert was asking for. Christie knew Robert, no matter how little time they'd had together. His big trooper needed touch right now.

"Christie…"

This time Christie silenced Robert, placing a gentle finger over his lips. He was careful not to press down on the split in Robert's lip. When the larger man obediently fell silent, Christie wrapped his arms around his lover as tightly as he could. He laid his head on Robert's shoulder and hummed one of his favorite old spirituals, then sang it softly into his love's ear. It had helped when Aunt Cate sang it to him after his mom and dad died, and he had used it to sooth himself more than once after the bombing.

Long the road,

We travel on our way home.

Long the road,

We keep travelling on.

We travel,

Travel on,

And travelling on,

Our weary souls are growing strong.

To travel on,

Travelling on.

Oh, then we ring them bells

Ring them charming bells.

Ring them charming bells.

Christie changed the lines in between. Instead of 'travel over Jordan', he simply sang 'travel on'. Christie was still singing it when Frankie woke and made her way into their bedroom. Robert hastily pulled the bedding up over Christie and himself. Frankie climbed up on the other side of Robert, humming an astonishingly beautiful, wordless descant above Christie's melody. Then Caro joined in. Robert quivered in his arms and Christie knew the big man had heard Caro's smoky contralto join them. A warm calm spread from Christie's center right out to his fingers and toes. Here, singing this song with Robert in his arms, he felt more at peace than he had since the day Jenkins died.

Ring them charming bells.

Ring them charming bells.

Let your weary soul grow strong,

An' ring them charming bells.

They finished the song, and a warm breeze blew past Christie to stir Frankie's hair with the scent of patchouli. Christie snagged a pair of shorts from the dresser next to the bed, sliding into them under the covers before he passed another pair to Robert.

"I'm listening now, Robert. Tell me about this…um… handfasting? Yeah? I want to know why you want it. I'm sorry I don't remember what you told me before. I'll do anything to make you happy Robert. Don't you know that?"

Robert looked up then. Christie caught his breath. Robert's eyes burned into him so hotly, his skin should have been steaming. Yes, Robert knew he owned Christie.

Christie pressed his lips against Robert's, light as the kiss of a wishing flower on the wind. "You do know."

Gran had always told him he was too proud for his own good. Letting Christie see how broken he felt from their failure to fully connect hadn't been a conscious decision.

It had just happened.

And it had been all Christie needed.

Robert had looked up to let Christie see exactly how deep Robert's need for him ran. Once he'd understood how much his young lover craved that, it had been easy to give it to him.

"Would you like to hear about the ceremony we're having?"

Christie's lips quirked up. He met Robert's eyes and started to giggle. Robert had to laugh as well.

"Okay, Christie, I get that I have to include you in the decision. Would you like to hear about the ceremony I'd like to have? Stop laughing. I'm gonna mark all your answers down as total agreement with everything I want if you don't take this more seriously."

Christie slid down to bury his chuckling face against Robert's chest. Robert had to grin at the sight. Frankie joined in, chortling at the sound of Christie's humor. She started adding in words, giggling out repeated choruses of Poppa and Daddy. It was clear Christie was Poppa, and Robert was Daddy. She took turns patting them as she said the words. After a few moments, Christie's stomach gave a loud rumble and she stopped to stare at it with big eyes.

"Maybe we'd better get some breakfast started, hmm?"

Christie nodded without lifting his head, rubbing his face along Robert's chest. Somehow Robert managed to get all three of them up off of the bed and through the hallway into the kitchen without dropping either Christie or Frankie. They'd both silently refused to let go of him even for the short time it took to walk into the kitchen. Once there he deposited Frankie in her booster seat. When her pretty rosebud lips started to pucker into a pout he shook his head at her.

"No pancakes for pouty babies, Frankie! Pancakes are only for smiling babies."

The little fiend fluttered her eyelashes at him and gave him a sweetly innocent looking smile.

He turned his head to look at Christie. The smaller man was still clinging to his side, legs wrapped around Robert's waist. Robert held him with one arm, sliding his free hand under Christie's chin to lift it up.

"That goes for you too, baby."

Christie grinned impishly at him. Then, the tease slid his legs down until one rested across Robert's crotch and one across his ass. Christie squeezed his legs together a minute amount. Robert grunted at the unexpected and unusual caress. Christie laughed, relaxed his legs until his feet touched the floor, and stood on his own.

"No pouting here, Robert. I adore…pancakes."

Robert narrowed his eyes at Christie. The little wretch wasn't playing nice. Using the slutty Christie voice with Frankie awake and in the same room was a clear declaration of war.

"I dunno Christie. You're a pretty bad baby. I think you might need a spanking."

Christie's laughter choked off as his eyes went instantly smoky. He ran a hand down his front as though unconsciously checking himself for visible signs of arousal. When his hand brushed across his burgeoning erection he hissed quietly. His eyes shot to Robert's. Mouthing the word, 'later', he quickly sat at the table. Robert turned away to make the pancakes feeling mightily pleased with his Collins handling techniques.

The care and feeding of this pair of Collinses was a tricky business at best. They were both too damned cute for their own good. It was tough being the only non-Collins in the crowd. A mew sounded by his feet. Well, except for Miss Kitty. She evened things up by being around, sort of. Robert chuckled quietly to himself as he heated the cast iron skillet and mixed the batter. Christie and Frankie were chattering behind him as she babbled to him about her newest teddy bear, and Christie responded.

"I…Caro," Robert whispered as he flipped the crisp golden cakes, "if you ever see my friend Cody, tell him I found what I was looking for. Tell him I'm happy."

A hint of a warm breeze touched his face. He smelled patchouli. For a second he gazed into eyes that weren't there, older, and infinitely wiser versions of Frankie's cerulean orbs. His breath stuttered in his chest. He knew Caro had just promised to pass the message along though she hadn't said a word.

He thanked her, and turned his attention back to his cooking. Robert hummed, flipping pancakes onto the platter once they were done, his brain busily planning out every detail of the coming ceremony that would unite them in the eyes of the rest of the world. Here, were it mattered, they were already a family.

The road was long,

But we travelled on,

An' we are al-ready home.

So ring those charming bells,

Ring those charming bells.

Well, they weren't the words Christie and Caro had sung, but in Robert's heart he knew they were the right words for what he had here and now. It was clear the song helped Christie, made him feel centered and calm. He'd shared that with Robert…so

Robert gave it right back to him infusing his voice with every bit of energy he possessed. It was a good song, and wrapping it in his energy was binding them together with a thousand gossamer strands of love.

CHAPTER TWENTY-FIVE

Christie watched out the back window of the farmhouse kitchen as deer sniffed the place where Petra Lindstrom had carefully laid brightly colored ribbons on the ground, outlining the edges of a circle. It was a beautiful spot for a wedding. The only thing stopping the day from being perfect was Evans' absence. Christie blew out a resigned breath. At least he had a few moments to come to terms with not having his best friend after Robert at his wedding.

The light tread of feet in the hallway alerted him that his reprieve was over. He was the only one up aside from Robert's mom, so it was no mystery who the person rustling around in the kitchen behind him was.

"Good morning, Petra."

Mrs. Lindstrom had looked up from the stove where she'd been just setting a kettle to heat. She pulled a second mug from the cabinet above her head and waved him over to the table.

"I've told you to call me mother, or mom, as the rest of my children do, haven't I, Christie?"

Christie's face burned. For someone with skin that was golden-brown even in the depths of winter, he blushed noticeably far too often. He nodded.

"Yes ma'am, you did. I-I thought I'd wait until I'm officially part of the family. After the handfasting it would feel more... right."

He tried not to fiddle with his coffee.

"Don't you worry that the animals will make a mess of your work?"

Petra glanced out the window past Christie's head. Her smile brightened, and she shook her head.

"No, the animals won't harm the circle. Their presence is a

blessing on it."

Well, as long as he didn't step in a 'blessing' during the handfasting, Christie supposed he could work with that. The coffee cup squeaked under his thumb.

Petra reached her hand out and patted his arm.

"Are you allergic to anything Christie?"

Christie lifted one eyebrow, arching it at her unconsciously. Petra arched her eyebrow back.

"Uh, I don't have any allergies that I know of. Not to any foods."

Christie gave Petra a nervous glance.

"Ah, Petra, am I going to be ingesting something … medicinal…during this ceremony? I really can't take anything illegal. The Army does surprise urinalysis tests you know."

Petra blinked at him. Then she shook her head in what could only be exasperation.

"I'd like to make you a bit of tea to soothe your nerves. It's just a bit of chamomile, nothing that would cause you to get in trouble with your Army."

Christie discovered that it actually was possible to shuffle in one's seat. He cleared his throat.

"I'm sorry, Petra. I just don't know much about all this… umm, Wicca stuff. I do know the Army would throw me out in a heartbeat for coming up hot on a urine test, even if I am their poster-boy for gay marriage right now."

The kettle whistled then, and Petra walked over to the stove to turn it off. She poured two mugs full of hot water and then brought them over to the table where Christie still sat. She set his down in front of him and from the basket in the center of the table, pulled out an ordinary Lipton tea-bag.

"Well, Christie, I don't think your Army has any problems with Lipton, do they?"

Christie smiled, shaking his head no. Petra pulled a sugar bowl and a pot of honey from the high sided wicker basket as well. She passed him both, along with a spoon.

"I'll leave the doctoring of it to you then young man. I have a few more things to prepare before people begin arriving, so I'll be taking mine with me. You just relax. Don't worry that you'll look foolish. We won't let you make any mistakes during the ceremony, I promise."

Robert was buzzing with excitement. The last time he'd felt this electrified had been the summer he'd gotten caught out in a thunderstorm. The tree he'd been sheltering from the rain under had been struck by lightning. He'd felt suddenly uncomfortable where he was and had been in the act of taking his first step away when the tree was hit. For days after he'd felt lighter than air. Robert grinned at his reflection in the mirror.

"Today, I'm running toward the lightning."

The ringing of the phone interrupted his happy moment of nonsense. He picked it up on the second ring, hoping to hear Christie on the other end. "Good morning, Lindstrom-Collins residence."

"I need to speak to Collins." Robert blinked at Sgt. Tarans' gruff voice on the line. Not only had Sgt. Tarans approved Christie's leave paperwork, he'd also been invited to the handfasting as a guest. The man had to know where Christie would be this morning.

"Ah, Sergeant Tarans, is something wrong?"

A grunt sounded over the phone. Robert actually recognized this one as Sgt. Tarans 'I'm sick to effing death of the bull the PR shits are pulling' grunt. Except if the old man said it, he'd actually say 'pukes' instead of 'shits'. Curiously, he would say 'effing' instead of 'fucking'. Go figure.

"Damned PR—they want the post commander to be present for the big Army wedding ceremony, and Major General LaVerson won't be available until October. I wanted to make sure you kids are having this done by a legally recognized minister or priest or whatever, so you're covered for housing. Collins needs to be able to change a lot of paperwork down at legal, so this ceremony needs to be one the state recognizes."

Robert heaved a sigh of relief. That wasn't so bad. Christie would be upset, but they could deal with this.

"Don't worry; my mom is a fully ordained Wicca priestess with full legal standing in the state of New York. I'll just give her a call to make sure she files all the right paperwork. Judge Wallace will be there too, so I'll ask him to sign-off on whatever she needs."

Sergeant Tarans grunted again. Robert didn't recognize this one. He heard the sound of Mrs. Tarans voice in the background then, and realized she must have elbowed the other man or poked him. There was another grunt and then he could hear her words clearly.

"Halbert, get off the phone. You've been on that thing all morning. We need to leave in half an hour and you haven't even started to get ready."

Robert grinned. There was no question as to who ran that household.

"Sergeant, I'll just let you get going. Sounds like you have incoming there."

Sergeant Tarans gave his, 'damn boy, that almost made me laugh' grunt. Then he hung up. Robert stared bemusedly at the phone for a minute, and then he laughed and went back to getting himself ready. He had to get going as well. He was picking Christie's Aunt Cate up at the airport in an hour and forty-five minutes. It was a thirty to forty minute drive to the Ogdensburg airport from here.

Robert had been expecting to have to pick Christie's aunt up in Syracuse until Christie told him she'd be flying herself out from California in a friend's Cessna. It appeared Aunt Cate was a woman of many talents. He finished getting dressed in the exact outfit he'd worn to the symphony with Christie. Then he went to feed Miss Kitty before he left for the airport.

Robert was glad he'd left a little early. The traffic on NY-812 North had been brutal. He'd had no idea Ogdensburg had some big festival going on this week. There was no helping the fact he was going to be nearly twenty minutes late picking up Christie's aunt. At least there'd been someone answering the little airports phone, so he'd been able to leave a message for her.

Pulling in and parking his car in the tiny lot, Robert started to make his way over to the small terminal at the airfield. A flash of something purple and green passed behind the building's window. Then the door was flung open before Robert had quite gotten to it. A slender woman with long silver hair pulled back in a messy braid came rushing out. She was taller than Christie, her skin more fair, her ethnicity clearly less varied than his sweet Christie's, but there was no mistaking the close relationship. They both had the upside down mouth with the big pouty top lip.

"Robert!"

Between Christie and Nikki, Robert was pretty sure he knew what to expect. He braced himself, opened his arms, and waited. He was right. Cate leapt the last few feet in a maneuver that showed remarkable agility for someone who had to be nearly as old as his dad. He caught her and chuckled.

"Aunt Cate. It's lovely to finally meet you in person."

The scent of patchouli engulfed him. He wasn't sure if it was Cate or if Caro had decided to get in on the reunion. Cate's hands fluttered over his back and then she was stepping back, silver bangles jingling.

"Oh, Caro, how sweet of you to come meet me at the airport." Cate beamed at the air next to his right shoulder. "Shouldn't you be with Christie though? You know he gets so nervous about things like this. Hmmm? Yes dear, you're likely right. No, you'd better not ride with us dear. There's likely going to be some very negative energy for a bit. No, no, nonsense Caro. You're particularly sensitive to it in your current discorporate state.

That's a good girl. We'll see you at the wedding dear."

She turned to Robert with a serene expression. Winding her long silk scarf thrice around her neck with one hand, she took his arm with the other. She urged him toward the terminal.

"Come along dear, we need to hurry and get my bags from the plane. I parked it right over in the hangar there."

Robert pulled the door open for her. Cate made her way over to a small pile of luggage. She picked up the top two bags, leaving the last two for him.

"I'm really sorry about running late, Aunt Cate. I had no idea there was some big festival up here this weekend. We'll take Route Eleven on the way home. That road should be a little clearer."

Cate smiled at him over her shoulder. She was already halfway to the door. Robert hustled to catch up to her.

"That should be fine dear. I phoned Evans when I got your message and told him to meet us at the gate. His car isn't working again, so I told him we'd just pick him up there. Nikki can give him a ride home tonight after the party is over."

Robert was so shocked he let the terminal's glass door hit him in the face without even attempting to stop it. Cate looked back at him and tsked. She set her bags down, pulled a gorgeous blue handkerchief out of a purse Robert hadn't even realized she was carrying, and made her way back to him. He thought, in his defense, the purse was made of the exact same materials as her... hippie dress. He didn't know if that was the right term. He'd have to ask Ally later.

"Focus, Robert. Your head is all over the place, and if you keep battering me with those Sherman tank thoughts I'll have a headache all through Christie's wedding. I know it's your wedding too dear, but Christie's my baby...you know how it goes."

Robert stood still and let her tend to his newly split lip. It gave him a moment to gather himself. It wouldn't do to start yelling at Christie's aunt.

"I'm your aunt too, Robert. Especially after today, hmm?

There, that's got you all cleaned up. Let's get these bags in the trunk and hustle down to Fort Drum."

Robert gaped after her. This time however, he managed to keep his thoughts to himself, as well as getting out the door without further injury. He waited until the bags were safely stored in the trunk, he was buckled into his seat-belt, and Cate was pulling hers across her shoulders.

"There is no chance in hell that I am allowing Evans to come to my wedding, let alone giving him a ride there."

Cate smiled at him sweetly. Oh shit. He knew that smile. Christie gave him that smile right before he hit him upside the head with his own stupidity. She released her buckle without latching it shut and started to open the car door.

"That's fine dear. I'm sure Christie will understand that I couldn't make the wedding. Evans did say he could come pick me up if this happened. The poor dear won't have access to a car until after four though. You'd better pop the trunk so I can get my bags out. I imagine after this you'll want me to stay in a hotel?"

She got out of the car and walked around to the trunk of the car. She was just standing back there, waiting patiently. Robert ground his teeth together. If someone could give him one good reason he should allow that licentious little prick to take part in his handfasting celebration…

Aunt Cate's voice came clearly through her still open door.

"I can give you three, Robert."

She was calmly getting back into the car and fastening her seat-belt. She acted like it was a foregone conclusion he would agree with whatever she had to say. He arched an eyebrow at her and waited. Cate held up her left hand, ticking the three points off on her fingers.

"One; you love Christie. Two; it will hurt Christie if that boy isn't at his wedding. Three; Eight words the Wiccan Rede fulfill; An it harm none, do what ye will."

Shit. She had him. Robert ground his teeth again and put the car into gear. He should have known. Christie had to have learned that frighteningly Machiavellian negotiation technique from someone. And hell, he'd just met Robert's sisters within the last year, so it couldn't have been from them.

Cate gave him twenty minutes to cool down. Robert used them to stew instead. After a while, he started to feel like an ass though. He took a deep breath. He'd try. Cate reached over and patted his arm.

"That's nice dear. I did have a nice long chat with young Mr. Evans. He understands he's only at the wedding on your sufferance, and he's promised to try not to do anything to piss you off."

Robert swerved the car. Cate chuckled. She patted his arm again.

"Do try not to wreck the car dear. I did see all three of us at the wedding, but I'd much rather get there in this car, and preferably without the excitement of an auto wreck. Did you think that old ladies wouldn't use words like 'piss off'?"

Robert bit his bottom lip. Shaking his head he decided that he'd best just throw in the towel with this Collins as well. He took his left hand off the steering wheel, reaching across himself to pat Cate's hand where it rested on his right arm.

"Cate, I surrender. I promise to behave with Evans as long as he behaves with Christie. I make no promises for my sisters though. I really have no control over them."

Cate chuckled. The woman was clearly demented. He'd seen many strong, brave men flee in fear before the massed viciousness that was a gathering of angry Lindstrom women.

"Don't worry about your sisters, Robert. Your mother will have them sorted out before we get there with Mr. Evans. He needs to be there as much as you and I do, and not only because of Christie. Goddess knows how long he'd muck around on his own otherwise."

On that cryptic note, Cate fell silent, closing her eyes and leaning her head against the window. Robert let her rest, figuring she would tell him more if and when she deemed it necessary.

Christie couldn't believe his eyes when Evans got out of Robert's car after Aunt Cate did. He squealed and ran out the front door of the farmhouse. Aunt Cate intercepted him before he leapt on Evans to hug the stuffing out of him.

"Go to your Robert first boy. He needs the reassurance."

Shuddering at the near miss, Christie took his Aunt Cate's advice. Robert met his eyes, and Christie was fiercely glad his aunt had made it look as though all his over the top excitement had been for her alone. The feelings he held for Robert were too big and too hot for his body to hold. He leapt on his lover and tried to kiss them all into Robert's gasping mouth.

"He was like this when we were overseas."

Evans's voice sounded a little sad, as if he were yearning, not Christie, but for what Christie and Robert had in each other.

"He was half a world away, and all he could see was this man."

Christie hoped Robert could hear that as well, because Christie wanted his friend back.

"He always was rather single-hearted."

Christie saw his aunt nodding emphatically at Evans. Snorting into Robert's mouth, Christie set them both to laughing. Trust Aunt Cate to mangle a popular saying and leave it making more sense than it had before she did. He lifted his head, unsurprised at this point to find himself held off the ground in Robert's arms. He winked at Robert and spoke before Evans could embarrass himself by trying to correct her.

"Just go with it Evans. It's much easier if you just go with it..."

Christie was still speaking when a sharp gasp from behind cut him off. Robert had set him down and moved toward whoever had made the noise before Christie could even get his mouth closed.

Oh shit. It was Nikki. "Dammit, Nalle, let me go. What is that piece of shit doing here?"

Christie bit his lip. He really didn't want them at odds. Shitfuckpissdamn. This was supposed to be love and crunchy granola/hippie/Wiccian Wedding, not a WWF match. Nikki was yelling, Evans had a pinched, unhappy look on his face, and—"Calm yourself, child. It is not for you to decide who your brother would allow at his wedding."

Christie jumped. He'd forgotten Aunt Cate was there.

Nikki stopped speaking at all. Her eyes sparkled with a mutinous glare, but her chest didn't seem to be moving at all. It took a moment for Christie to see that rise and fall. Good. At least Aunt Cate's powerful voice hadn't stopped her breathing.

Evans was way too appreciative of Nikki's assets. He was not what you'd call a subtle guy…but this was over the top for him. It was like he wanted someone to notice his overt appreciation. Fuck. Christie had to get him out of there before Robert spotted him right into a hospital bed.

"Ummm…Robert?"

Okay, not too bad. A little squeaky, at the end maybe but that couldn't be helped. Robert would mark that down to being upset over the commotion.

"Yeah, baby?"

"Uh, why don't I take Evans and Aunt Cate to meet your mother before the ceremony, so she can explain stuff to them, and you keep your sister here until she calms down? I'd hate for Frankie to see her like this or even hear her aunt talking like that."

Robert nodded his head. Nikki looked both pissed and apologetic. Evans looked horny. Almost too horny. But then, Evans usually looked horny. Christie rubbed his temples and hustled Evans and Aunt Cate around the corner of the house. Once he was sure they were out of ear shot he smacked Evans as hard as he could with the back of his hand on Evans's thick chest before collapsing onto the stairs to the side porch.

"Christ on a cracker with jalapeños and cheese, Evans. Do you have a damned death wish? If Robert catches you looking at his baby sister like that, he'll kill you. Twice!"

Evans snorted at him.

Then he made a big production of nudging Christie's side with the toe of his very shiny boot. Well, shit, if he wanted to change the subject that badly, Christie could roll with it.

"Evans! You shined your boots for my wedding?"

Evans growled at him, his expression warring between apparent relief at the change of topic and irritation at the pristine state of his boots being pointed out. Christie was touched. Evans never shined his boots, not even for first sergeant inspections. The only time Christie had ever seen Evans's boots shined was when he thought his dads were coming to visit. They'd had some emergency at their job and been unable to come, but still, it had made it clear were Evans's priorities were. He only shined for loved ones.

He grinned up at Evans. Evans tried to look pissed, but he couldn't hold it. A smirk crept up on one side of his mouth. Christie scrambled to his feet and caught Evans in a big hug. Christie'd been longing to give his friend some sign of affection since the second the silly fucker had stepped out of Robert's car.

"You're my best friend Evans, after Robert. And by the way, I'd shine my boots for you too man…"

Christie let his voice trail off. He waggled his eyebrows at Evans.

"…so, not exactly gay, huh?"

Evans shot him a dirty look before he answered.

"Not completely bent, no."

Christie chortled over that description.

"Uh, Evans, I think the 'incident' showed us that you're not exactly straight."

This time Evans pouted. Christie rolled his eyes. He rolled his hand, urging him to spill.

"Maybe kinda-sorta a little bent."

"Okay buddy, we'll go with bi-way beyond-curious for now."

Evans smacked the back of Christie's head.

"Christ on a cracker Evans, don't you have any manners? You don't abuse the groom on his wedding day."

Evans appeared to consider that. A smirk crept across his face. He even snickered as he answered.

"Except at a collaring for a BDSM couple."

Christie rolled his eyes and led Evans in the direction his aunt had disappeared in.

Robert stood with Christie at the edge of the circle. The tingly electric feeling had returned, and every bit of it started and stopped in the beautiful man standing by his side. In the distance he could hear voices, but their meaning was entirely lost on him. All he could see was the prominent curve of Christie's upper lip, the way his non-regulation hair fell from the crown of his head to just touch his eyebrows. Christie's smile was a touch strained. Robert lifted Christie's hand and kissed the back of it. Christie caught his breath and his eyes darkened. One voice rose above the rest.

"Robert? Son, stop distracting your groom. Come on into the circle."

The guests laughed at that. Robert took his eyes off Christie long enough to note it was indeed time for them to enter the circle. He guided Christie around the circle, whispering "clockwise" when Christie started to pull in the wrong direction. They stopped in front of the altar.

His mother must have cast the circle while he was marveling at the color of Christie's eyes, because the next thing Robert knew his brothers and sisters were calling out in their turns, each from their quarter.

"East, O Air I ask blessings of wisdom on Robert and Christie and their union."

"South, O Fire I ask blessings of passion on Robert and Christie and their union."

"West, O Water I ask blessings of love on Robert and Christie and their union."

"North, O Earth I ask blessings of stability on Robert and Christie and their union."

Then Robert's mother's voice rose like a beautiful song. She called down the blessings of the Lord and Lady, and sealed the circle. Robert's focus had all returned to Christie. He traced with his eyes the new little scar at the corner of his love's mouth. Christie had not yet been able to tell him about it. He ached to touch it with his tongue.

Christie reached forward, taking a bit of cake in his hands, breaking a small bite off with his lips. Robert reached to place the bite back on the altar, and then Christie handed him the cake and they reversed the order. He had written such beautiful vows for Christie, but when the time came for him to speak the only word he could say was the name of the man standing at his side. He had no idea what Christ had said to him.

Rings and ribbons and leaping over a sword came next and the sword he remembered, because Aunt Cate had flown herself so she could bring it all the way from California. It had been Christie's father's sword, and Christie had cried when he saw it, remembering that it had been his father's favorite of all the swords in his collection. Then someone unbound their hands but Robert kept Christie's clasped close in his.

Voices buzzed and the circle was open, but never broken.

May the gods preserve the Craft and may the Craft preserve the gods. He mouthed the words he heard being chanted in the background, so Christie would know what they were.

They left the circle to join the boisterous crowd. Robert kissed Frankie and passed her back into his mother's arms and then he picked Christie up and did what he'd been longing to do for hours. He kissed his husband with his whole will, bringing all the love he'd imagined flowering between them for the rest of time. He kissed his love until the entire world melted away and there was only Christie, there was only Robert, and bright and hot between them a shining love.

Butcher, baker, candlestick maker...ummm, eww, every chance she gets and she surely would if these damn characters would ever shut up. Born in West Palm Beach, Florida and raised...er, is all over the damn place a sufficiently descriptive term? No? Then how about this? Tinker, tailer, Indian chief...Oooo, especially when smexy men are involved(!), only under duress, and did the cheek-bones give it away?

Seriously? Cherie has lived in Washington DC, Virginia, Upper Michigan, Texas, New York, California, and Alabama in the United States; Hessen in Germany, London in England, Masirah Island in Oman and sometimes it was a house, sometimes in a tent and sometimes anyplace she could find to lay her head.

She's been in love with words since before she drew breath, and doesn't see that every changing. She writes stories. Sometimes she writes music with them, sometimes they're poems, and lately to her great delight, m/m erotic romance. Yum. Smexy man to the second...or third power...now that's the kinda of math she can get behind!

The hair curls or frizzes as it will, the eyes are green and tend to look in two different directions - no, really- and the rest is subject to change. You know the guy who didn't know if he was a butterfly dreaming he was a man or a man dreaming he was a butterfly? Yeah, that's her, but substitute drag queen for butterfly and wacky, wild ex-Army chick for man.

Trademarks Acknowledgment

The author acknowledges the trademark status and trademark owners of the following wordmarks mentioned in this work of fiction:

A-1: Kraft Foods Holdings

Astroglide: Daniel X Wray

Bailey's: R & A Bailey & Co

Cessna: The Cessna Aircraft Company

Coke: The Coca-Cola Company

Dancing Bull: E. & J. Gallo Winery Corporation

Fancy Feast: Carnation Company

Good Start: Societe des Produits Nestle

Kahlua: The Kahlua Company

Lipton: Unilever Supply Chain, Inc

Little Caesars: LC Trademarks, Inc

McDonald's: McDonald's Corporation

Neon: Chrysler Corporation

Nike: Nike, Inc

Obsession: Calvin Klein Cosmetics

Post-it: 3M Company

Sugar Creek: Wilson Farms-Ahold Corp

Yankees: New York Yankees Partnership

SERVICEMEMBERS LEGAL DEFENSE NETWORK

Servicemembers Legal Defense Network is a nonpartisan, nonprofit, legal services, watchdog and policy organization dedicated to ending discrimination against and harassment of military personnel affected by "Don't Ask, Don't Tell" (DADT).The SLDN provides free, confidential legal services to all those impacted by DADT and related discrimination. Since 1993, its inhouse legal team has responded to more than 9,000 requests for assistance. In Congress, it leads the fight to repeal DADT and replace it with a law that ensures equal treatment for every servicemember, regardless of sexual orientation. In the courts, it works to challenge the constitutionality of DADT.

SLDN
PO Box 65301
Washington DC 20035-5301
On the Web: http://sldn.org/

Call: (202) 328-3244
or (202) 328-FAIR
e-mail: sldn@sldn.org

THE GLBT NATIONAL HELP CENTER

The GLBT National Help Center is a nonprofit, tax-exempt organization that is dedicated to meeting the needs of the gay, lesbian, bisexual and transgender community and those questioning their sexual orientation and gender identity. It is an outgrowth of the Gay & Lesbian National Hotline, which began in 1996 and now is a primary program of The GLBT National Help Center. It offers several different programs including two national hotlines that help members of the GLBT community talk about the important issues that they are facing in their lives. It helps end the isolation that many people feel, by providing a safe environment on the phone or via the internet to discuss issues that people can't talk about anywhere else. The GLBT National Help Center also helps other organizations build the infrastructure they need to provide strong support to our community at the local level.

National Hotline: 1-888-THE-GLNH (1-888-843-4564)
National Youth Talkline 1-800-246-PRIDE (1-800-246-7743)
On the Web: http://www.glnh.org/
e-mail: info@glbtnationalhelpcenter.org